domino

DOMINO BOOKS LIMITED

I expected the manager to be a hard geezer, but this one was round and soft all over. She swayed in wearing a cute black number and bounced over to the desk, parting her glossy red lips in a golden smile.

'The girl's only new,' she said, making a nice little flourish with her treble chins. 'But she'll understand what men like soon enough. Just give me twenty quid, ducks, and you can go down and see the lady with the scar.'

MADAME EDDIE'S
CHAMBER OF HORRORS

By
MIKE SHELLEY

Madame Eddie's Chamber of Horrors
is an original publication of Domino Books Ltd,
Edenderry Industrial Estate,
326/328 Crumlin Rd, Belfast BT14 7EE

© Mike Shelley 1984
ISBN 0 946963 01 0

Typeset, printed and bound in Northern Ireland by
Brough, Cox and Dunn Ltd, Clifton St, Belfast.
Set in 10 on 12 Century Textbook.

Cover and Design by Triplicate,
Linenhall St, Belfast
Illustration by Tony Bell

I'M NOT SAYING I WOULD HAVE WENT OFF WITH THAT BAG

The private detective business was slow that week. On Monday morning it was so private I just sat in my office and filled up two ashtrays with the butts of my handrolled. Apart from beating up a gypsy who tried to pick my pocket down at the lunchtime boozer, I did nothing all afternoon except roll up some more fags and wonder who had rearranged the stick-on letters on my door.

I'd been after him for some time. I hadn't minded PRIVAT DETECTIVE or PIRATE DETECTIVE or even PRIVATE DEFECTIVE, but then he started to get fancy and come up with stuff like EVE VICE TIRED TART and his latest effort:

```
        E
    CAT
        T I
        E
        DIE
        V
        PERV
```

So I decided to do a bit of rearranging myself when I caught him, i.e. his face, and he'd know to his sorrow what it meant to fool around with an IRATE DETECTIVE.

About 4.30 a small baldy man called McConkey came in and asked what those letters meant under B. H. HUGGINS. I asked him if he'd ever heard of a person having letters after his name. He said he had, but nothing as complicated as those.

'You ever hear of organic chemistry?' I said sneeringly, pointing for him to take a chair.

He nodded and looked impressed. Clients like aggressive private eyes because they don't like paying out good money to some jerk who can be pushed around or fobbed off with a sobstory.

'Alright then,' I said. 'What's your problem?'

His little pig eyes clouded over and his chin started to quiver. I thought he was going to snivel. He said in a rush,

'My wife's been keeping some very bad company and I'm afraid that something injudicious might happen.' He sniffed and handed me a photo.

I knew what he meant by 'injudicious' when I cast my eye over a brunette in her early thirties whose eyes held a hint of a promise that the rest of her would have no problem at all in keeping.

6

I had to smile. It's always the bad company that's to blame. It's never because the chick wants more excitement than a baldy little fusspot with a droopy dick can ever give her.

I said, 'So she's fooling around. What do you want me to do about it?'

'I thought perhaps you.... you would know.' He bent over with his head in his hand and started to cry.

I felt sorry for him. Being aggressive was one thing but making your clients cry was another. I told him I'd do what I could. I nursed the details and fifty quid out of him then walked him to the door with my arm over his shoulders. Poor sod, he'd never heard about not having honey guarded by a bear.

Sorting out McConkey's wife was small beer compared to my usual cases, but I was glad of it after going through a lean period following my brush with the C.I.D.

'You're heading for the big one, Huggins,' I was told as they pushed me before the judge. But he soon wiped the smiles off their faces when he called me an innocent victim of circumstances who didn't know those fivers were forged. Which in all fairness I think he would have said anyway, even if I hadn't sent him a snap of himself slipping out of a callgirl's flat.

Anyway, there I was this night, back in business, and standing well back into the darkness of this entry up Molloy St. in Clapham. It was a cold night and I was just going to stamp around a bit and get myself warm when a light appeared in the window of this basement. I opened the gate without a sound, moved like a commando towards the window, and peered in.

There was this tart in the room. She was sitting in a large tiled fireplace, one foot at either side of the fire, and poking vigorously at the glowing remains. She was probably cold because she was wearing only two towels, one wrapped round her head and the other round her waist.

While I was looking at this I heard a car move off from the house opposite. I ran to the gate and saw a Rover disappearing down the street.

'Balls,' I shouted, becoming mad with myself. That was the house I was supposed to be watching, and now my suspect had got clean away and I didn't even know if McConkey's wife was with him or not.

Suddenly I heard screaming from behind me. I turned round and saw that sexpot at the window. She yelled,

'Charlie, come quick, there's a peeping Tom!'

I didn't want to stick around to meet Charlie, so I opened the gate and ran off into the night.

I was walking briskly towards my own apartments, and still thinking about that bit with the poker, when I heard a cry of anguish and a loud shout of 'Help!' I couldn't see anything in the dark so I advanced up the street in the direction of the sounds.

As I neared this narrow entry I heard another cry, and quickly turning down it I came upon two ruffians duffing up this old boy. Viciously I lashed into them, unleashing terrific punches at their jaws and solar plexuses, and it wasn't long before they scurried off with a couple of boots up the backside to help them on their way.

'Oh, I can't thank you enough,' moaned the old geezer. 'They were after this money and now you've saved it.'

He was lying on the ground, clutching a shopping bag, and as he tried to get up I could see it was packed with £ notes and fivers.

I told him, 'That's too much for an old duffer like you to be carting around at night in this district,' and as I was thinking of freeing him from the cares of safeguarding such an amount, he made it easy for me by passing out and falling in a heap.

I'm not saying I would have went off with that bag, but I never got the chance because at this moment two cops descended upon me and ordered me against the wall. With my fingertips against the brickwork and my feet spreadeagled, they proceeded to frisk me.

'Shit,' I said. 'It was me who came to his rescue.'

But to no avail. I was bundled into a police car and whisked away. For the second time in six months I was in handcuffs. (The third, counting that time in Lisa's establishment in Kensington when I was getting the treatment from a lush female.) But this time I was speeding off to the tender mercies of a lush cop called Sgt. Mungo with a robbery with violence charge hanging over me or even worse if the old geezer croaked it.

The car drew up. I was shoved into the station and then left, still handcuffed, in a small 'interview room' with a watchful copper.

After a while Sgt. Mungo came in with a smile all over his chops. He gave a roar and there was so much whisky in it I could almost name the brand.

'On your bleeding feet, soldier!'

Sgt. Mungo had been a sergeant in the army too. So had I, but not in a cushy H.Q. company like him. It's funny how the rear echelon units usually produced the worst bullies.

I got up, he sat down and the constable went out.

9

He lit a cigarette, still smiling and gloating. He said, 'Ye're a stupid bastard, Huggins.'

I said, 'Stupid's not the word, Sgt. Mungo. I'm positively thick.'

'Don't be cheeky, soldier.'

'What's wrong with you?' I asked. 'I'm only agreeing with you.'

'Aye, but it's the way ye're doing it.'

I went to sit down.

'Hold it, Huggins!'

Hell, you'd have thought I was going for my gun. 'Alright,' I said, 'I don't need this then,' and I stepped to one side and kicked the chair across the room. Then I rattled my cuffs at him.

Sgt. Mungo jumped to his feet and shouted for the constable. The door opened.

'Crack his bloody heid in, he's attackin' muh.'

But it was a plainclothesman who stepped in. He took in the situation at a glance.

'Sit down you,' he said calmly, looking at me. 'Alright, Sergeant, you can go now, and take those cuffs off that man.'

Sgt. Mungo unshackled me, protesting that I would go berserk, then left in a sulk. The young detective sat down and threw me for a loop by not asking about the old geezer at all.

'When'd you last see the Captain?' he asked nonchalantly, pushing his hat back and rubbing his forehead.

Now that was a good one because nobody had seen the Captain for over two years, although I knew the cops were still after him for that tickle down the West End. In fact, I thought I was putting one over on the Captain when he was away in Hamburg and me sleeping with his wife, Eddie. But all the while she was after the plan of the security lay-out of this jewellers on Oxford St. which had somehow found its way into my pocket.

Of course, I'd no intention of going on a job like that so I stuck it for safekeeping into issue 49 of *Sophisticated Sex Life*. Then, after Eddie had left, I found it was missing and that was very irritating because it ruined my complete set.

'Well over two years ago,' I said.

'Tell me about it.'

So I did. I went into the same long yarn I gave them the last time. The questions came fast and thick but I tried to stay master of the situation, and even yawned a few times. I told it high-key, low-key, jokey, I told him how the Captain kept Eddie locked up all day because she went with men. I told him irrelevant stories and lies within lies. Anything at all to keep the spotlight away from my accidental role in the robbery. I had him completely baffled.

He asked a few more half-hearted questions then said,

'Piss off, Huggins.'

I stood up and put on my hat.

'The old dozer's put me in the clear, then?'

He nodded. As I opened the door I could hear him say softly, as if to himself, 'I still think you were on that Oxford St. job, Huggins.'

I just smiled and went out.

BLOOD FLOWED QUICKLY AFTER WE PLAYED 'THE MARSEILLAISE'

Mornings aren't a good time in the private detective business. One time I decided to find out what they'd be like without a hangover but they turned out to be even worse. I just sat there listening to my ears ringing, and swatting at flies that were floaters in my eyes, and every now and again my liver would give a polite little cough. It was all very unnatural.

Around one p.m. I phoned up McConkey's wife, but she wasn't in. I set out to look for her, making a tour of the afternoon clubs he'd mentioned, but I couldn't find her.

There were no clients waiting for me when I got back to the office — which was just as well since I was anything but sober — so I just put my feet up on the desk and tried to figure out why the cops were resurrecting that Oxford St. job.

It was after seven when I woke up, and I had to rush home because this bloke who said he was an international violinist was coming to my apartments that night. He had heard that the old fiddle hanging with no strings on my living room wall was a Stradivarius.

He arrived promptly at eight. Harriet, my current girlfriend, who had been a protégée of mine since she got out of Holloway, let him in. I was sitting in my armchair by the fire, feeling the effects of several good whiskies.

'Mr. Huggins,' he said, 'it's so thrilling to come across such a piece at any time, but particularly so under such inauspicious circumstances.'

I put my hand up to my face and winked at Harriet. I took off my hornrimmed specs, polished them on my shirt, put them on again, gave him an open-eyed stare and said,

'Explain yourself, Mr. Mantovani.'

'My name is Manley,' he said, 'and I'm referring to your violin. I thought you were aware of my keen interest in it.'

'You see that violin?' I said, looking up at it. 'I bought it years ago off a gypsy who didn't know what it was worth. Of course, I spotted the Stradivarius trademark straightaway, but I didn't tell him that. The gypsy didn't think it was valuable but he said it was and tried to take a rise out of me by asking £9 for it.   So I looked him in the eyes and hypnotised him and took the violin out of his hands like you would take a bottle from a baby's mouth.

'Well, he tried to clean me, so I cleaned him. Wasn't I right?' I leant towards Mr. Manley and peered intently at him. 'Well, wasn't I?'

13

He nodded and looked away. I continued: 'My old man taught me the violin and by the age of 20 — no, 17 — I was a . . . a maestro . . . would that be the word for it?'

He nodded again, then said, 'I thought perhaps —'

I cut him short. 'A fellow came in the other night, from the British Museum he was, and he was wanting me to play for them. He was sitting just where you are now and I played a medley from Bach, and he said he couldn't believe it. I don't play like anyone else, you know. Well, Mr. Moneypenny, how's old Stradivarius doing? The last report I had, he was over 80 and living in Russia on drugs.'

I jumped out of my chair. 'If you think that violin is good, wait till you see this.' From behind the armchair I pulled out my mandolin-banjo. 'This is a genuine Mendolsohn, you know. I suppose you heard that I was the only man in Ireland who could double-up on the banjo. That's what brought you here, wasn't it? It wasn't the Stradivarius at all. Takes a lifetime to learn, you know.'

I stood in front of him and played 'The Marseillaise'. I winked at him.

I said, 'That's one thing my family have always been strong in, and that's French Revolutionary songs. We certainly know our French Revolutionary songs, so we do. In fact, long ago in history when my family went round Ireland with hatchets, beheading unsatisfactory characters, we always played "The Marseillaise". Yes sir, blood flowed quickly after we played "The Marseillaise".'

I replaced the mandolin-banjo in its case, then sat down. 'Are you interested in rare books, Mr. Manual?'

Reaching over, I removed a paperback from my library — two shelves on the wall beside my armchair.

'First edition, it is. Was offered money for it only last night. Now, would this be what you've really come for?'

'No, I'm not a collector of books,' he said wearily, handing back the book — which was a J.T. Edson western — and getting to his feet. 'I'm afraid I must go now. It's getting quite late. Thank you for showing me the violin — and, of course, how to double-up.'

'Not at all,' I said, and Harriet saw him out. She came back with an enormous grin on her drink-blotched face.

I said, 'I hope I didn't show him up too much. After all, I have been playing longer.'

'And another thing,' I added. 'You might have given him a drink or a cup of tea. I don't know what he'll think of us.'

Harriet plonked her rear on the arm of my chair. 'I'm in two minds myself,' she said. 'What was the reason for all that?'

'It was only a tactic,' I explained, 'to put Manley on the wrong foot. I don't know what he's after, but I'm danged sure he's not an international violinist.'

HER HOT SMOKEY BREATH WAS
STEAMING UP MY GLASSES

The next afternoon around three o'clock I drove over to McConkey's house in Chelsea. I'm sure I saw a female face at one of the upstairs windows as I strolled up the path. But whoever it was, she was determined not to answer the door. So I went down the street to a call box and dialled her number. After the twentieth ring I replaced the phone and strode back to the house.

I must have kept my finger on that door bell for at least three minutes, until finally I gave it up and started back down the path. Looking up, I saw that face again. It had a cross expression and it definitely didn't belong to McConkey's wife. I didn't know what to make of this, so I got into my Riley and drove back to Clapham.

When I arrived at my apartments they looked very

untidy and I'm sure poor Harriet's ears must have been burning after I let forth a few choice comments about her not tidying up after I went to work. Then I noticed that the drawers had been rifled and I realised that somebody had been in looking for something.

My first thought of course was for the Stradivarius, but it was still there, hanging on the wall. I hung my hat over it then went out to the kitchen and put on the electric kettle to make a cup of tea.

I started to watch a film on the T.V. about the Korean War. I was interested in this because I had seen action there myself and it wasn't a very pleasant sight. But the sorrowful thing about this movie was that all the Americans were dressed up in W.W.2 uniforms. I wondered at the amount of money they'd spent on this film for it to be so hopeless. Droves of commies were being mowed down when a knock came to the door.

I didn't recognise her at first because the last time I'd seen her she wasn't wearing a scar that almost bisected her left cheek.

She came in like she owned the place, threw her fur coat over the settee, made a snide remark about the room looking very lived in, and then asked for scotch, water not lemonade and no ice.

I apologised that I only had Bushmills Irish and could she see her way clear to accepting that?

'Don't be sarcastic, Barney,' she said and looked into the kitchen, the bedroom and the spare room. She was wearing a green nylon blouse and a short black skirt that allowed glimpses anytime she did anything except stand still or walk in a straight line. This was Eddie, wife and principal agent of the man I once knew as the Captain.

She sat down in my armchair by the fire.

17

I said, 'Make yourself at home, sweetheart.'

She crossed her legs and suddenly there was nothing in the room but thigh and nylon. I gave her the whiskey and a cocktail cigarette, I even lit it for her.

She said, 'I'm glad you're pleased to see me.' Then she made a face and threw her cigarette in the fire. 'That's awful. Stale as hell.'

It probably was. I'd had the packet for ages. Even Harriet wouldn't smoke them. I said,

'You're looking better than ever, Eddie.'

She smiled and we made small suggestive talk for a few minutes. Then I said,

'How's the old Cap doing?'

That's when her expression changed. She took on a look of determination. She said,

'He's in a jam. He's been remanded.'

'Remanded?' I echoed. I knew what the word meant alright. 'It's not like the Cap to be brought up.' Then I had a horrible thought. 'It's not for that Oxford St. carry on, is it?'

'No, it's not, and that's what I'm trying to avoid. The cops have him in for fraud, but fortunately they still don't know who he really is. He goes through names like nobody's business and until now he's never had his prints taken. This is why it's tricky. We've got to get him off this rap without revealing his real identity.'

'We?' I repeated, putting down my glass. That's when I realised I had to watch myself. I knew Eddie from the old days and I knew that, like most women I've ever known, she was a dangerous liar and very cunning. 'We?'

Her head was bent. She ran her ringed hand down over her eyes and the scar. Then she looked up, fixed me with a stare, and the room seemed filled with a hard cold blue. She said slowly, as if explaining things to a halfwit,

18

'It should be perfectly clear to you that if the Captain goes down for this it will be only a matter of time before the cops put two and two together and come up with the Oxford St. job. And if they make him talk about that one, which they usually can do, that means they come up with several other people, including you.'

That's when I got mad. I said, 'Maybe I am a bit slow on the uptake about these things but would you be so good as to explain to me this one little minor detail? The haul from that Oxford St. jewellers was at least two hundred grand, so if I was in on the job why was it that not one bleeding penny of it ever came my bleeding way?'

She looked up at the ceiling. 'I always wondered about that myself.'

'I bet you effing well did. I bet you worried about it so much you went right off your boiled lobster and the Captain had to buy another mink fur coat so as to cheer you up.'

She drained her glass and held it towards me. 'You **are** in a sarcastic mood tonight, Barney. Not so much water this time, if you don't mind.'

I gave her a dirty look then I went into the kitchen and poured two drinks. When I came back she was unbuttoning her blouse. She was very weighty in that region, big and comfortable. I admired her effrontery. She wasn't making any bones about it. No manoeuvring or subtle plays. Just an acre of white thigh set off tastefully against the black lace of her briefs and two almost grotesquely big boobs that danced like elephants as she pushed me down onto the settee and sat on my lap.

After her tongue had made two or three circuits of my face and her hot smokey breath was steaming up my glasses, she was riding about two inches higher and I was feeling intensely open to suggestion.

She whispered, 'By an odd coincidence, Barney darling, the judge who's trying the Captain is the same one you had. The word is you put the fix in and I was just wondering . . .'

'You're on,' I said. 'I'll tell you how I did it.'

Ten minutes later I was in the bedroom getting undressed, glasses and all. I'd just put the heater on when she came in, rubbing her arms and complaining that the lino was cold. I just shrugged and pulled back the cover.

'Take your hat off, Barney,' she said and started to shiver.

NONE OF THEM WEAR SEAMED STOCKINGS OR HATS WITH A VEIL

The next morning Eddie was looking daggers at me over the breakfast table. Unfortunately, she wasn't logical enough to grasp the simple fact that telling her how I fixed that judge was not the same thing as giving her the means to fix him again.

But it didn't worry me because I was used to dirty looks, particularly from women. Harriet had a good line in them herself. Hers were more withering than murderous. It would have been interesting to see her in action against this one. I was quite good myself at browbeating scowls and open-eyed stares, but there was no way I could even approach the evil-eye class they were in.

Eddie said, 'You'll be sorry, cock.'

I replied, 'I'm not running a photo-agency in blackmail pictures, you know. You must be awful soft if you thought you just had to strip and I'd hand over the results of three days hard surveillance and undercoverwork.'

She snorted. 'Any time you're in disguise you're probably hiding from your own clients who want to know why you haven't come up with anything.'

I poured her another cup of tea. 'The truth is, it's my clients who wear disguises. Not moustaches and false noses and suchlike, but they seldom tell me their real names.'

'I guess you're just that kind of detective.'

'One for highly delicate work, you mean?'

'What about, for delicate work that doesn't require a pedantic concern for legal niceties?'

I snubbed out my handrolled and got to my feet. 'I think you've hit the nail on the head, Eddie.'

She said, 'What about getting me that photograph?'

I said, 'I'll wander on down to the office and see if that piece I'm expecting has turned up. The way I'm expecting her, she'll be sitting in the waiting room smoking a Turkish cigarette and wearing seamed stockings and a hat with a veil. Then she'll rise from the haze, blowing smoke rings, and her voice will be husky when she says, "Come, Huggins, let me take you away from all this. My father, the Sultan, has need of a Chief of Private Detectives —" '

'I can think of some other people who will want to take you away from all this, and none of them wear seamed stockings or hats with a veil, at least not on duty. Besides, I was down at your office yesterday, looking for you, and you don't have a waiting room.'

'It's open-plan. Did you like my new sign?'

Eddie nearly choked on her tea. When she stopped coughing she said,

'You're getting worse, Barney. There were three people looking at that when I arrived. We were all trying to figure out what it meant.'

'Damned if I know either. There's a fella does it for me, and I hope he'll leave it alone for a while because it's impressed one client already.'

I put on my hat and went to the door. I said,

'Don't bother turning the place over again, because it's not here. I'm not saying you can't have the photo, but it's going to cost you. I don't accept that if the Captain goes down he'll spill the beans on the Oxford St. job.'

I got into my Riley and drove to the office. It was 10.30 and I didn't have a hangover. There was a red Mini parked in my spot. I had a feeling it was going to be one of those days.

The landlord was shaking his head at my new sign. I did a sharp but silent about-turn, which didn't help me one bit. He seemed to know every move I made. I've always said landlords would make good detectives.

'You know what day this is, Huggins?' He'd long since dispensed with the Mr.

There was an obvious answer to that but there was no point in pushing it. 'We're in luck,' I said. 'I'm on a well-paying case at the present time.'

He didn't seem too impressed. I gave him £40 out of the £50 I'd got from McConkey. He'd long since stopped accepting cheques. His bloodshot eyes looked up from the money and went from me to the sign to the ceiling. They seemed to have a pitiful look in them. He turned and made his way slowly along the corridor. He seemed a lot older than when I first moved into that building. I decided to cheer him up.

I called after him, 'You never know, if I get some more clients I'll be able to pay you in advance each month.'

He didn't reply, but as he shuffled away I noticed his shoulders were shaking slightly. He was either laughing or crying.

SHE LIKED TO DANCE TO SWING MUSIC AND PIANO ROCK

Sometimes when I'm waiting for a client or lunchtime to arrive I sit back and become very thoughtful. I wonder why I do certain things that even I know at the time are not very sensible. Things like taking Eddie down to the Bunch of Grapes that evening while knowing full well that Harriet would likely be there.

Anytime you saw Harriet in the street she was either coming back from the Bunch of Grapes or going to it. She even got mail addressed there. She'd put down a carpet in the last snug on the left and brought in pictures for the wall. Even the manager and barmen used to knock on the batwing doors and ask if they could come in.

As I led Eddie to the last snug some of the regulars

looked up awestruck at my audacity. Thinking they were gaping at her face, she asked them sharply if they'd never seen anybody with a scar before. I stood behind her and said it was the fur coat they were staring at, and started to nod. They took the hint and assured her humbly that they were only admiring her style.

I was fascinated by Eddie's scar, though I still hadn't asked her how she got it. The scar tissue was white and slightly raised from the skin. It contrasted delicately with her shaggy black hair and enormous lips. It had a lot more character than the burst blood vessels on my own cheek, though I'm sure that wouldn't have been much consolation to her.

I said, 'Five hundred for the picture and that's the lowest I'm going.'

I got the cold blue treatment again, then there was a flash of red as she flicked a finger at me.

'I hope you're left alive to regret this.'

I said, 'What's that supposed to mean?'

'Why don't you use your imagination?'

I said, 'I am, and it's killing me.'

She raised her penciled eyebrows. I wasn't sure what I meant either. Perhaps it had something to do with the five-inch heels of her green leather shoes. One of which was pressing down onto the toes of my right foot in a very determined fashion. Or perhaps it was connected with my bladder's sudden signal about those two bottles of stout and three cups of tea. Or perhaps it was just hearing Harriet's sweet voice floating effortlessly above the din of the pub.

I said, 'I'll be right back.'

'Let's go in here, darling,' I said to Harriet, guiding her by the elbow into the first snug as you came in the door. 'Petesy's been sick in the end one, you see.'

26

Petesy Marker was my casual assistant. He was almost an expert on the Fulham and Clapham underworld. He was short with a weasel face and usually wore a checked suit with oil stains on it. Petesy was astute and very cheap.

'That's a terrific hat,' I told Harriet as she plonked herself down on the bench in the snug. I stood there for a moment admiring its faded blue felt, its attractively frayed brim, and the way it was tilted to one side, almost obscuring her right eye and ear. It went well with her smeared red lipstick and the run in her left stocking. But that's not faulting her hat, because I'm a connoisseur of smudged bright make-up and ladders in nylon stockings, particularly above the knee.

Harriet said, 'That's the one you bought me for my birthday last year. It's the first time I've worn it.'

I said, 'It really stands out, that hat does.'

'Yes, they don't make them like this anymore.'

I said, 'Well, that's that. What are we having?'

'The usual.'

'Alright. Back in two ticks.'

Harriet's usual was a bottle of strong lager and a whiskey. So was it any wonder that I decided last year to put my foot down and make her buy her own drink?

She refused point blank to do this, so I was forced to acquire a music centre for my apartments in order that she would spend more time inside. I used to get the drink cheap from one of Petesy's pals and she liked to dance to swing music and piano rock.

She used to get pretty excited waltzing and jitterbugging around the room. That was okay with me because she wasn't doing it in public and making a fool of herself. I think she preferred it that way too. Sometimes I would even dance with her myself. We'd turn down the lights and smooch around the room to songs like 'Sweet Lorraine', 'That Old Feeling', and 'Just The Way You Are'.

While I was chatting to Emily the barmaid, Petesy came in wearing a black beret and a raincoat that was several years overdue for a drycleaning.

'I'd like a word with you, Mr. 'Uggins,' he said softly.

It wasn't softly enough to prevent an aroma of fried onions and curry from crawling up my nose, but his tone indicated he had certain information and that meant I'd be well advised to buy him a drink.

'Pint?'

'Ta, Mr. 'Uggins.'

'Grab that table by the door and I'll bring it over.'

Emily set up a pint of bitter, a lager, a whiskey, a Bacardi and Coke, and a dark rum for me. She said, 'What's got into you tonight?'

I said, 'It's Harriet's treat. I've never seen her so flush.'

'She come into something?'

'Naw, she's gone back to her old game. She always said this was a good spot for it.'

'And what's that?'

I smiled. 'I think she calls it professional dating.'

Emily gazed at me with her mouth open wider than usual. Then she screwed up her nose and the skin rose in tiny waves below her eyes. As usual, Harriet was not be disposed of that easily.

'Go on with you. This is a respectable place. They'd want something more impressive than Harriet here.'

I always thought that Harriet was good for Emily. She stimulated her normally sluggish brain to great feats of reasoning.

I gave Emily a fiver. After checking the number against a list hanging above the liquor bottles, she gave me a pound and two very small coins. If I couldn't get rid of at least one of my camp-followers I was going to find myself very short. I wondered if Emily would let me back on the slate.

I put the drinks on a tray that advertised Cherokee Ale and made the rounds discreetly. A young man with large ears asked me for a pint of lager and a barley wine and to bring him change for the juke box. I said, 'Why not? I'm buying for half the pub as it is.'

Eddie said, 'I thought you were dead.'

Harriet said, 'Did you have to go into Fulham for these or what?'

Petesy said, 'Ta, Mr. 'Uggins.'

I took off my jacket and sat down with my back to the bar. I put my snap-brim on Petesy's head and put his black beret on mine. It was too small to go on properly so I adjusted it to a rakish angle by looking into my silver cigarette case. I got a false bushy moustache from the pocket of my jacket and used the cigarette case to put that on too.

Petesy said, 'We don't often see you going into disguises in 'ere, Mr. 'Uggins.'

'I should use a phone box, you mean?' Petesy was always making little digs at me. Coming out with innocent-sounding statements and questions and jokes with hidden jags. But I always outsmarted him by replying in a way that kept him in doubt as to whether I had caught on or not.

I said, 'Let's have it, then.'

Petesy made a display of looking into an obviously empty packet of Woodbine and being disappointed at finding nothing there. I snapped open my cigarette case

29

and said,

'You seem to have run out.'

Petesy was quick, but when it comes to palming and sleight of hand I'm nobody's fool. He had one in his fingers and one in his palm when I made the mistake of saying,

'Sure that's enough for you?'

'That's very kind of you, Mr. 'Uggins,' said Petesy and proceeded to half fill his Woodbine packet with my handrolled.

I said, 'Now will you tell me what you've found out?'

'I will, Mr. 'Uggins,' he said and drained his pint.

'Well?'

'There was this bloke down the Crown that was asking about you.'

'So?'

'Somebody said I knew you and he came up and bought me a pint.'

'And?'

'A pint of best bitter it was.'

'That's interesting.' I reached him a pound. 'Here, get yourself one in. No, I insist. It's definitely my go. Some other time perhaps.'

'Ta, Mr. 'Uggins.'

'What did he want to know?'

'Where you lived mostly.'

'Did you tell him?'

He looked hurt. 'Course I didn't. Told him you went to Australia, didn't I? Just like you always told me to say. I tell you, Mr. 'Uggins, I was a bit fearsome about telling him that 'cause he looked a right 'ard geezer. Even me pint was shaking—'

'Ach, it's the soldier. Ah might have known.'

I picked up my glass and polished off the rum. But

there wasn't enough of it to make any headway against the sinking feeling that had come over me. Perhaps, I thought, Harriet just wasn't being nasty when she said it's always my nose that gives me away when I go into disguise.

I glanced over at Petesy. He was sitting with his head down, trying to hide under my hat.

EDDIE CAME OUT OF THE BATHROOM
LIKE A WET FURRY COBRA

All good detectives know that you can easily fail to realise that something is missing simply because you completely expected it to be there. So while I was sitting hunched over the table it was probably my past experiences that made me assume Sgt. Mungo was rattling on in his normal abusive way. But when I did finally get round to actually listening to what he was saying, I discovered he was talking about getting laid in Pusan, Korea, and falling off pontoons in the Injun River. Which was interesting enough, but if he'd been up with the fighting he'd have got laid in Pyongyang and fallen into the Yalu River, as I did.

So I chanced a look up at him and there he was swaying gently in a double-breasted grey flannel suit and the great slabs of his cheeks fairly shining with bonhomie, whisky and an extra-close shave.

I'd kept the silver cigarette case in my hand so that I could see what else was happening behind me, and whenever I saw a flitting image of a grotesque shape with a blue felt hat on, I'd give Petesy a kick and he'd sink further into the snap-brim hat.

I whispered to him, 'Go into the first snug and tell Harriet (a) you were sick in her home from home, (b) I was arrested fifteen minutes ago, and (c) Sgt. Mungo has come to lift her for soliciting. She'll know what you mean.'

I said to Sgt. Mungo, 'That was some action you saw over there, so it was. Let me get you a drink, you deserve it.'

At least Emily didn't recognise me. I brought two shorts along to the last snug and backed in through the batwing doors.

I said quickly, 'You wouldn't believe the narrow escape I have just had . . . Now, where were we?' I sat down and stuck out my left foot. 'Why don't you try the other one this time?'

Eddie was still staring at me. She said, 'I'd made up my mind to let you have it with this . . . ' She showed me her knuckleduster. 'But now I don't have the heart.'

'I know how you feel,' I said. 'I once caught my ring on this fella's teeth when I was hitting him and it nearly broke my finger. By the way, is that your heavy that's going around asking questions about me?'

'By the cut of you, you're the last person who should be taking the piss.'

'I have my reasons for this. In fact this rig-out saved me from a nasty confrontation tonight.'

'With the heavy?'

'That's as good a word as any.' I knocked back the rum. 'Come on and drink up and let's get out of here.'

I helped her on with her fur coat. She said,

'I spent a lot of time tonight staring up at that picture. What is it?'

'That's an aerial view of Holloway. I gave it to a certain person for Christmas. She likes to sit in here and work out complicated escapes.'

'Going to spring somebody, is she?'

'No, in case she goes back in. She's one of the greatest criminal minds in this entire area but she's sometimes ahead of her time. It was an ingenious plan to try and draw two thou from Major Darlington's account when he was standing behind her in the queue but it turned out to be too subtle for her own good.'

'Sounds like a right one.'

'Yes, a real winner. Even Sgt. Mungo said it was a pathetic case.'

Petesy looked up admiringly as I hurried Eddie out. Sgt. Mungo was sitting with his arm round him, singing 'Auld Lang Syne'.

In the first snug there were four empty glasses, a smell of cheap perfume and a message written in red lipstick on the wall.

ILL SEE YOU LATTER

When we got back I took out my mandolin-banjo and knelt before her and sang, 'When You Were Sweet Sixteen'. She was so choked up she had to bury her head in her fur coat that was hanging over the back of my armchair by the fire.

Then I stood up and gave a lively recital of 'The Black Velvet Band' and 'The Yellow Rose Of Texas' to

34

cheer her up. I was halfway through 'South Of The Border' when she said it was about time she had a bath and washed her hair.

I was getting quite fond of the rich smell of her hair and armpits, so I said,

'The water's all rusty.'

'That's alright, I'm not going to drink it.'

'Save the water,' I said, 'I'll be in after you.' I handed her the fur coat. 'Put this on when you come out. There's no point in getting dressed this late.'

The scar made a beguiling wriggle as she gave one of her rare smiles. Her teeth were perfectly white and had a sort of natural unevenness that made them look almost real. She licked her lips, draped the coat over her shoulders, then jerked her hips a few times. As she sashayed towards the bathroom she said,

'The Captain likes that too, poor dear. But he knew better than to treat me just as a sex object.'

I bet he did, I thought. I'd heard from Petesy how she even used to rob the Captain blind. In fact, I wouldn't have put anything past her when it came to thievery or double-crossing people.

The taps had just stopped coughing and splurging when there came a knock on the door.

It was a tall bloke wearing a raincoat and a peaked cap. He invited himself in with a shiny big revolver, then asked politely if he could speak to Eddie.

'Eddie's not here, mate,' I said in a voice that was meant to be loud but came out as a high-pitched croak.

By this time I had backed as far as my armchair and the mandolin-banjo, and when I saw the bathroom door opening slightly I knew I had to distract his attention. I said,

'I should show you this because this is what she

came for. You never know, it might mean something to you.'

As I started to play 'The Marseillaise' Eddie came out of the bathroom like a wet furry cobra. I was hitting wrong notes all over the place as she advanced in slow motion with an earthenware po poised over her head towards a polite gunman who now had a tic twitching under his left eye.

He was saying, 'That's enough of that,' just as Eddie, with a great sweep of her breasts, was bringing the po down onto his becheckered dome.

He never knew what hit him. His knees buckled, his arms flew up and he jerked around for a couple of seconds like a puppet on a string. As he was doing this, Eddie skilfully bonked him again and this time he did a little shuffle on his knees before closing his eyes and rolling onto his back.

Eddie rubbed her bare foot over his face to see if he was shamming. Then she turned to me and said,

'This here used to be the Captain's minder. Then he turned turk and damned near shopped the whole organisation.'

I lit up a handrolled, inhaling deeply.

'I've got to hand it to you, Eddie, there's definitely more to you than being a sex object. That was as terrific a piece of sneaking up as I've ever saw.'

She knelt down, grabbed his hair and gave his head a shake to see if he was still out.

'You made it easy,' she said, getting up. 'He was mesmerised at you playing that tune in a lopsided beret and a moustache half peeling off your lip.'

I said, 'What are we going to do with him?'

She sighed. 'There's only one thing we can do.'

I told her straight, 'You needn't ask me to help you

with that. It's far too chancy.'

She said, 'I don't mean do him in. I mean we'll have to keep him out of circulation until after the trial's over. Then we'll give him to the Captain.'

I said, 'That's alright then. I didn't think we should let him go so that he could come back and do the job properly on us.'

She gave a sneering smile. 'I told you you were involved in this but you wouldn't believe me. Go and get some rope and a gag.'

I wasn't at all sure I would have been involved in this if she hadn't arrived on the scene. But I didn't want to say anything to annoy her, because thinking of her performing that heroic exploit with nothing on but a fur coat was giving me all kinds of ideas. I went out and got the rope and the gag.

WE CAN'T HAVE HER RUNNING AMOK
THROUGH IT ALL

The clock-radio woke me up at half eight with a discussion on French turkeys. I keep it on Radio 4 because the last thing I need at that hour is a load of happy patter from a D.J. I think that's in bad taste when you wake up feeling like one of the living dead.

Since mornings aren't a good time in my business, I snuggled up into the bust of the warm female beside me and went on with my dream about drawing on Callan in a hushed Bunch of Grapes.

Two hours later I brought Eddie a cup of tea and her packet of Players. People with shaggy hairdo's don't look all that different in the mornings. She said,

'Better ask what's-his-name if he wants one too.'

I'd forgotten about him. I put on a false beard and

wig and went into the spare room. 'Cup of tea?'

He was either nodding eagerly or shaking with anger.

I loosened his gag a little. 'Sugar?'

Even through the gag it came out as a roar. 'I'm gonna do you, mate.'

'Now don't be like that,' I said, shutting him up again. 'That's no way to talk to somebody trying to bring you a cup of tea in the morning.'

As I closed the door I added, 'And after me remarking to Eddie how well mannered you were last night as well. Even she had to admit you were a nice talker.'

After putting on my wide-brimmed hat and greatcoat, I said to Eddie, who was still in bed,

'He might have shopped you but I don't want you working him over in here. Leave all that to the Captain.'

'If he ever gets out,' she snapped, giving me a crusty blue glare. 'And you'll be to blame if he doesn't.'

That's another fine gem of logic, I thought. I said, 'We'll talk about that tonight. In the meantime just keep tight and stay sensible. Okay?' I picked up my camera and went out.

At three o'clock I was standing outside this club in Soho. There was a large metal grille over the front door and inside this stood a giant black wearing a fur coat. People wanting in had to show him a card before he would open a door in the grille.

About half three McConkey's wife came out with a redhead and two black dudes. I managed to get a picture before they went off in a taxi. The idea was to follow her, but the steady stream of taxis that had been passing for the past half hour suddenly came to a complete end. So I had to let her go. I wished I had brought my Riley but it's very tricky finding a parking spot in Soho these days. I think they should have special places set aside for detectives.

One thing I did discover though was that there was somebody following me. All the time I was outside the club this bloke was hovering around the area. If he looked in one shop window he looked in a hundred. After McConkey's wife had sped off, I walked towards him in order to get a good look at his face. But he was wearing a soft hat and a muffler, and before I could get near him he scurried off down an alley.

When I got back Eddie was holding the tall heavy's nose so that he would take a drink.

'What's that?' I asked.

'Just a mild sedative. The bloke's overwrought.'

'Been playing you up, has he?'

She stood up. 'Well, he hasn't much scope but he's been doing his best.'

I tut-tutted at the heavy. 'Come on, Eddie,' I said. 'Let's have a shot.'

We went into the living room. I poured two whiskies. Eddie was still wearing the same black skirt and green blouse she'd arrived in two days ago. I don't think she'd even washed her smalls. I thought of that saying about the fur coat and no knickers. I had to smile as I watched her smooth down her skirt after she crossed her legs like a professional woman and then with her lips pursed she took delicate little sips of the whiskey.

She said seriously, 'You're being a proper bastard not giving me that photograph, you know. I wouldn't have believed that anyone could be so greedy and self-seeking when his mate's in trouble.'

This from her? I thought. One of the foremost female gangsters in London? The same one who was perfectly happy to make me the prize dupe for the Oxford St. job? There's a word for people like her and I was trying to think of it when she added,

'Surely you can do one decent thing in your whole life without asking money for it?'

I said, 'I don't owe the Captain anything except a bloody good hiding. He's played some sore tricks on me in his time and you must admit that. If he needs the photo he'll pay the market price for it and that's final. He's only himself to blame.'

'But I've told you before, we don't have any ready money. Whatever we have is all abroad because of what that jerk in the next room did to us.'

In my game you can't fall for sobstories. I said, 'Well that's just hard lines on the old Captain then. Either you produce the necessary or the Cap goes down. You've got a few days yet. Shouldn't be too hard for a looker like you.'

Her eyes widened and her mouth dropped, but it was all theatrics. 'You mean?'

'Don't act the injured virgin. You were on the game while it was still one of the sunrise industries. Half the broads I've ever known have been on it at one time or another.'

Needless to say, I got the cold blue treatment again. She picked up her cigarettes and stomped into the bedroom, slamming the door. I'd an idea there was a bit of trouble in store for Barney Huggins Esquire — but I didn't think it was coming quite so soon.

I was sitting in my armchair watching a western, remarking to myself that the Texas Rangers were wearing Mexican War uniforms, when I heard the door opening and who should land in but Harriet herself.

I'd always regretted giving her that key, but when

you're feeling romantic you do daft things like that. At least I never went as far as some blokes and signed joint leases or even opened joint bank accounts with them. You'd have to be very romantic to do something like that.

I might have had some trouble finding the word for Eddie's mood, but a glance at Harriet's face told me instantly what was on her mind. The words didn't just spring to mind, they shot out of her eyes like fireworks. An emblazoned **Angry Suspicion** seemed to fire the air between us and I said into it, casually,

'What happened to you last night?'

She didn't reply, she was too busy sniffing the air and glaring at the two glasses and the fur coat draped over the settee. She even looked in the ashtrays and discovered Eddie's butts with the lipstick stains on them.

It was when she stood still and stared at the bedroom door that I became really nervous. Harriet was a hard case alright, but that Eddie could beat a man. Once Harriet went in there blood would flow and I had a good idea it wouldn't be Eddie's. There was even the possibility they would gang up and take it out on me.

The inspiration, if that's the right word, was sudden. I said,

'I'm more overjoyed to see you than I seem because I was planning a surprise and now you've almost spoilt it. This bloke from the market was here delivering what I'd bought you. In fact he's only just left. Yes, love, I've got you a new fur coat.'

Of course, I knew as soon as I said it that I had overstepped the mark. I was already thinking up plans for getting it back off her when she rushed at me and threw her arms around my neck.

'Oh Barney, how could I ever have doubted you?' she cried, planting wet kisses all over my face, including my glasses. 'Oh lover, forgive me. I'm a bad bad woman. You're too good to me. It's wonderful. I don't deserve it.'

She let go of me and put on the fur coat, whirling round in it and squealing. I took off my glasses and was cleaning the lenses when a blurred black and white shape rushed past me. There was a grunt, an almighty crack and then a thud. When I finally got the situation into focus, Eddie was rubbing her fist and glaring down at Harriet who was lying on the carpet.

I said, 'There was no call for that.'

Eddie knelt and started to pull Harriet out of the coat. She looked back savagely.

'Wasn't there? You think I was going to let her clear off with my fur coat?'

'It was only a ploy. I'd have got it back for you.'

'Sure you would. This coat's the only decent thing I've got left and you want to make ploys with it?'

'I still think you came on too strong.'

'Balls,' she said. 'Get me a drink.'

I came back with two whiskies. They seemed to take the edge off things. She said,

'I was ripping mad before she came in. Then when I heard you giving her my coat . . . well, that was the last straw. I just couldn't believe it.'

After lighting a cigarette she added, 'Besides, I recognised her voice. I knew that lady when I was working down the West End. We had a lulu of a run-in at one time and I still owed her one.'

I said, 'Well, I didn't know that. I suppose you do have a point.'

She said, 'What are you going to do with her?'

I put down my glass. 'Surely you're not thinking

of . . . ?'

She shrugged. 'It's up to you. But what's going to happen when she comes round and sees her old enemy sitting in your armchair wearing almost nothing but the fur coat?' Leering archly, she opened the coat to reveal her smalls.

My mind was a blank. Sometimes when thoughts are too horrible the mind is merciful enough to cut them out.

She added, 'Look at it this way. We're all in a tricky predicament at the moment, what with the Captain, the photo, the cops, etcetera, and we can't have her running amok through it all. She will, you know.'

Well, she was right there. Harriet was a sucker for punishment when it came to causing rows. She would keep on acting up and harping about the coat until she forced Eddie into giving her more thumpings. There was a case for putting Harriet into protective custody and I decided to look at it that way. I went out and got some more rope and another gag.

After I put her in with the tall heavy in the spare room, I used some of her red lipstick to write on the door,

MADAME EDDIE'S CHAMBER OF HORRORS

REAL DETECTIVES HAVE MORE
SENSE THAN THAT

The next morning about 11.30 I went out looking for McConkey's wife in my Riley. I'd been having some trouble with second gear, which I got round by changing directly from first to third, but it still came as a surprise when the whole gearbox seized up. I was sitting at a light on the Lavender Hill when it happened. After the drivers behind me had blared their horns through three light changes, I just got out of the damn thing and walked smartly off. It was on its last legs anyway.

That bloke from the day before was still following me. I picked him up at lunchtime as I was strolling down to the Bunch of Grapes. He was staying about fifty yards behind me all the time. He didn't seem to know that the first rule of following is to be mostly on the other side of the street.

As I'd expected, Petesy was already at it. After softening him up with a couple of pints, I gave him three quid and told him to be outside my apartments at eleven the next morning. His briefing was to follow the bloke in the soft hat who was on my tail and find out where he lived.

On the way back to the office I picked up the latest issue of *Sophisticated Sex Life* . They'd done themselves proud with this copy, featuring some of the best shots I'd seen in a long while. I placed it on the desk and then wheeled back in my chair in order to bring out their thighs. The best way to look at a pin-up is to lay it flat then stand back and contemplate it from a small angle. Most men don't know that.

I was going through it a second time, reading the ads and letters, when a hard geezer in a sheepskin coat stepped in and wanted to know if I was B.H. Huggins. After I decided I wasn't him at all, but was in fact his landlord who was also waiting for him, the geezer sat down in the visitors' chair by the hatstand and said he didn't mind waiting either.

While we were waiting we started to chat about things in general and I was relieved to hear that he was only from the Abel Finance Co. He mentioned that he'd started working for them that morning, this being his first assignment. He added that the secretary warned him not to be too hopeful, because if he did get anything out of this Huggins fellow he'd be succeeding where everyone else had failed.

I thought it was a dirty trick to give a new employee such a difficult task, so I told him to keep a stiff upper lip and gave him a tip on how to fiddle his income tax.

I left him still sitting there and walked back to my

apartments. Wherever she'd been, Eddie didn't return until almost midnight.

I said, 'Look here, Eddie, if you want prisoners you're going to have to look after them. They haven't been seen to for at least seven hours.'

I hadn't fed them, because it was agreed that she could keep them in the spare room only if they didn't know I was involved. The false beard and wig might have fooled the tall heavy but it definitely wouldn't take in Harriet.

She took off her coat. She was still wearing that black skirt and green blouse. She said,

'Alright, don't fuss me. I'll attend to them after you get me a drink.'

After she'd done her chore and had a couple more whiskies, she stood up and stretched, saying,

'You needn't think you're lying with me, Huggins. Not after what you said last night.'

I said, 'Suit yourself, sister,' and I think I meant it. But after she'd made a tantalising display of parading back and forth in her smalls from the bathroom to the bedroom, I went in and said I was prepared to knock twenty quid off the price of the photo. I didn't like having to pay to sleep in my own bed, but that settee would have started my bad back playing up again.

Eddie was up and ready for the road when I left before eleven the next morning. Having already decided to follow her, I stationed myself in the doorway of the flats opposite. As I had expected, the bloke with the soft hat was looking into a shop window about a hundred yards down the street. Beyond him, on the other side of the road, I caught a glimpse of Petesy's black beret.

After ten minutes, Eddie emerged and set off in the opposite direction from Petesy and the other one. She was walking with her head down, slightly stooped as always, but at a good pace, her high heels fairly clacking on the wet pavement. I let her go for fifty yards then stepped out into the light drizzle. When she reached the corner I made a quick glance back to check that we were all there.

There was a tricky moment on the Lavender Hill when a bus came along seconds after she arrived at the stop. We all had to run for it, with Petesy of course having the furthest to go. As he sat wheezing and coughing behind the bloke with the soft hat on the top deck, I made a mental note to mention to him about drawing attention to himself.

She got off the bus at Leicester Square. It was no surprise to me when she crossed into Soho, but I was taken back when I saw the handwritten sign on the street door of the shabby building she entered. It read,

Miss Eddie

Gents Tailoring
Collars and Cuffs
Room 3A

That didn't sound like Eddie at all. Still, if she wanted to make money doing that, it was nothing to do with me. I led the procession around Soho for a bit, just on the off chance I would bump into McConkey's wife. Then I got tired of that and gave the bloke in the soft hat the slip by the simple expedient of jumping on an underground train at the last possible moment.

Petesy was in the Bunch of Grapes at two o'clock. He was sitting on his own in the corner, nursing a flat pint. I've often remarked that Petesy wouldn't have had a drink problem if he made do with the little he bought himself.

I said, 'How'd it go?'

'Easy as pie, Mr. 'Uggins. 'E's living in this hotel in Paddington.'

'Did he tumble you?'

Petesy's eyes flashed up at me. He started to say something then thought better of it. 'Naw, not that one.'

'Come on then,' I said, 'get that lot down you, we've got work to do.'

Most of the work seemed to be involved in helping Petesy up six flights of unlit stairs to this bloke's room in Paddington. It was a mystery to me how somebody so out of condition could claim to be good at following.

I banged on the door and shouted, 'Open up in there, this is the detectives.'

He wasn't wearing his soft hat and muffler this time. In fact, he was looking pretty snazzy in a black suit and green bow tie. I pushed him back into the room until he was sitting in a hard-backed chair by the bed. Petesy closed the door then stood with his back against it, his finger bulging out his raincoat pocket.

I said, 'Well, if it isn't Mr. Manchester.'

He said gruffly, 'Manley's the name and well you know it. Don't let's have a repeat of the other night.'

'We won't,' I said, 'we'll try something different,' and I swiped him several times with the back of my hand.

He tried to get up from the chair, so I gave him a slight tap on the chin with my elbow. I said,

'Do you take me for a lug or what? I knew straight off you weren't an international violinist. It was sticking out a mile. What's your game?'

Surprisingly, he looked more sad than scared. He

49

said in a low voice,

'I'm an investigator working on an assignment. To disclose details would mean betraying my client's trust. I'm sure you can understand my position.'

'Tommyrot,' I said. 'It's only Philip Marlowe who lets his face get busted in rather than disclose details. Real detectives have more sense than that. What do you say?'

He said, 'I deceived you only about my reasons for wanting to see your violin. The sole purpose of my visit was to verify my client's claim that it was in fact a Stradivarius. More than that I will not divulge.'

I said, 'You mean it really is a Stradivarius?'

'Yes, it is precisely what you said it was.'

I gave a small whistle. Stradivarius was just a general term I used for an old violin, but now it seemed I had been right all these years without knowing it. I said,

'Are you sure I can't persuade you to tell me more about this?'

He shook his head. I turned to Petesy.

'You want a bash at making him talk?'

Petesy shook his head too.

I said, 'Well, search him then.'

When Petesy had finished searching, I said to Manley,

'Don't think you're off the hook yet, bub, because you're not.'

Petesy opened the door for me and we proceeded down the stairs. I said,

'Hand it over.'

He kept on going, so I stopped him with a hand on his shoulder. In the dark stairway his face was a yellow mask of innocence.

'I don't get you, Mr. 'Uggins.'

'Leave it off,' I told him. 'I saw what you took from that bloke's wallet. Half will do. Though, properly speaking, I should get it all because you've already been paid.'

'Yeah, all bleeding three quid of it,' he moaned, his hand reluctantly entering his raincoat pocket.

'And no looks neither,' I added as he pulled out the first crumpled fiver.

YOU CAN TELL YOUR WHORE
TO COME OUT IF SHE WANTS

The two prisoners were weighing on my mind a little bit, so the next evening I asked Eddie if we could transfer them to her new place in Soho.

'Quite impossible,' she said from my armchair by the fire. 'They're staying here until I get the photograph. Don't forget it's you who's dragging this whole business out.'

I said, 'What I'm thinking of is that after you clear off with the photo I'll be the one who's left in a tricky position. I mean, I'm sure Harriet and the tall heavy will be anxious to find out the reasons for all this.'

She had been swinging her green leather shoe from her toes. Now, with a sharp flick, she sent it hurtling at my head. When it missed, she took off the other one and

52

threw it at me. It bounced off the wall onto the floor.

She said, 'I'm tired of this. I'm particularly tired of hearing you whine about those two in there. I've told you before, the Captain will be looking after his ex-minder, which just leaves the girlfriend for you. Surely you can manage that on your own.'

'If he does come for him,' I said. 'And it's not whining to be looking at things realistically. It's all your fault that I'm in this situation. I was quite happy minding my own business until you came along and started cracking people on the head. It's a good job we don't all adopt that approach to life. Society would be a complete shambles if we did. Even the cavemen —'

'Oh sure,' she snapped. 'I should have let him shoot me and let her waltz off in my good coat. Don't forget it was you who tied them up.'

I said, 'What's done is done. We've now got to be more constructive about things . . .'

At this point there came a knocking on the door. I said, 'Into the kitchen. Stay there unless I give you a shout. Above all, keep your hands to yourself.'

I got rid of her empty glass and tipped her ashtray into the fire. As I opened the door I was expecting trouble alright, but it still came as a very stark shock to be gazing upon the squat features of a woman I'd made every attempt to forget about. Yes, the wife had finally tracked me down.

She didn't say anything, just barged on past me, her shoulders swinging in a very determined manner. She hadn't seemed to age much over the past five years, but there was no knowing what she was like under that cake of make-up. Her hair was definitely blacker than I remembered.

The first thing she did was kick Eddie's shoe along

the carpet. 'You can tell your whore to come out if she wants. Indeed, I'm glad to see you have one, for it'll be helpful to me when I'm telling the judge about all these years you haven't sent me a cold ha'penny, though from what I'm told it's at least two fancy women you're keeping at the present time...'

I realised too late she was making a bee-line for the Stradivarius. With a gasp of triumph she seized it from the wall, holding it against her chest.

'This is mine. Take a step towards it and I'll smash it against the wall, I swear I will.'

I said, 'Of course it's yours. Wasn't I keeping it there for you all this time? Do you think I wouldn't have sold it if I hadn't been? Sit down over there like a good woman and we'll work out a system for paying what I owe you.'

'Ah, I know you. You'll never change unless you're made.'

'That's precisely the point,' I explained. 'If you're taking me to law you'll definitely be asked if you gave me a chance to work things out. I've even got a witness that I asked you... Come on out, Eddie.'

Eddie stepped out, looking bored. The wife gave her a vicious once-over, probably storing up details for her description of the tramp I was living with.

'This is the wife,' I announced, and Eddie's response was a mixture of a snort and a snigger. Then there was a nice moment when I caught her eye and we both started to smile.

'Get us some drinks,' I said.

I turned to the wife. 'Sit yourself down. In fact, I was remarking to Eddie only the other night about turning over a new leaf.'

'You never know,' she said fair-mindedly. 'Even

rogues and gobshites like you have been known to mend their ways.'

'There's hope for us all,' I said, and Eddie came back with the drinks.

'Prosit,' I said, and the wife took a taste of the whiskey, then had a larger sip. It was her favourite drink.

It was interesting watching the knock-out drops take effect. Her voice dropped to a bearable tone and she began to grin. I think that after a couple of minutes she was seeing me and Eddie in roughly the same way as I look at things without my glasses.

Eddie said, 'I thought you didn't approve of this approach.'

I replied, 'You heard what she was going to do. Do you realise how scarce Stradivariuses are now? They're crying out for them all over the world.'

The wife said, 'What'youse mean by this approach?'

I said, 'We're stuck with two of them, another one won't matter. Might as well get hung for a sheep as a lamb.'

It's not easy concentrating on private detecting when you're living with Eddie and have three dangerous prisoners in the spare room, and that's why I suddenly decided to take a much more direct approach with McConkey's wife.

It was still before nine when we tucked the wife away, so I asked Eddie if she'd like to earn twenty quid.

'It's up to thirty now,' she said. 'I'm not going through that rigmarole again for a penny less.'

I said, 'No, it's concerning a case I'm on,' and I told her about McConkey's wife.

She said alright, and after I'd popped out and phoned up to make sure she was in, we set out on the bus for McConkey's house in Chelsea.

'Remember,' I told her in front of the door. 'Make a bloody good scene, and if you get into trouble give a sharp blow on the whistle.'

I stood back into the shadows as she rang the bell. The idea was of course to have Eddie make out she was the wife of one of McConkey's wife's boyfriends. If Eddie couldn't scare her, nobody could.

Ten minutes after she'd burst in there was still no sign of her, though I had heard quite a bit of yelling. So I put on my false beard and slipped in myself through the slightly open front door.

When I peeked into the large sitting room my first thought was a regret I hadn't brought my camera.

McConkey was sitting on a couch, trying to mop up the blood that was trickling down his face. Eddie was standing hands on hips under the chandelier, the light reflecting off her knuckleduster. A grey-haired man in a woollen suit was standing next to her, drawing out notes from his wallet. And a well-stacked woman was on her knees before him, crying, and wailing 'Oh please, Alex, I promise I'll never see him again.'

In all fairness to Eddie, though, the woman did look quite a bit like McConkey's wife. They were both between five foot and five foot seven, they both had long hair, though this one's was brown instead of black, and they both had good busts and wore lipstick.

The man said to Eddie, 'As you've just heard, she has no intention of seeing your husband again. I trust this will be sufficient compensation?'

As Eddie was stuffing the wad of notes into her bra, I backed off and went outside to wait. I hoped Eddie didn't think I was letting her keep that twenty pound I gave her.

She was looking quite pleased with herself when she came out.

I said, 'How'd it go?'

'Just as you planned. Though I think you might have cleared your plan with McConkey first. He didn't seem at all happy.'

'Who all was there?'

'Just the two of them.'

'Don't bother lying,' I said. 'I saw that bloke giving you money. I also saw that woman and she wasn't McConkey's wife.'

She stopped walking and put her hand on my arm.

'Barney, you're starting to annoy me again. You assured me that she was there, and as there was only one woman in that house I took it to be McConkey's wife. And don't talk to me about photographs, because women like that change their appearance as often as you change your socks.'

There was an obvious reply to that jibe, but I decided not to make it. I've never liked to annoy women when it came to within an hour of bedtime.

I ROLLED AND WRESTLED AND GAGGED LIKE A MANIAC

The next morning as I was making the tea it seemed to me that I'd got myself into a prize situation. There was a whole mess of stored-up trouble in the spare room, and Eddie had made more money out of looking for McConkey's wife than I had.

It seemed a tempting idea to simply clear out and leave Eddie in the lurch, just as I left my Riley on the Lavender Hill. Maybe I'd leave Clapham altogether, I thought. Take a great leap away from debts and heavies and Eddies and never come back. I knew I was broke alright, but until I started on my own again I could walk into any detective agency in the country with no problem. I decided to think about it.

I placed Eddie's tea on top of the radio and made a

last grope at her through the bedclothes. She opened her eyes, rolled over and said 'Bugger off.' Then I put on my hat and greatcoat and went outside to wait.

When she still hadn't come out after half an hour I went down to Greasy Annie's for another cup of tea and a bacon sandwich. I thought it was a rum case to be spending more time watching my own apartments than anywhere else.

Around eleven she came out in her fur coat and click-clacked her way towards the Lavender Hill. When she turned the corner I went down my steps, opened the door silently then slipped into the kitchen and smeared a couple of blobs of tomato sauce onto my hairline. Next, I opened the door of the spare room a little. All was quiet. As I tied my feet and hands with rope I shouted, 'No, Eddie! Have mercy!' and 'I'll get you for this!'

After I pushed the gag down into my mouth I threw myself against the door and plunged into the spare room, hoping they wouldn't notice me closing the door with my feet. For a while I made a great show of struggling against my bonds, rolling over and raging into the gag. Then I lay still and looked up for the first time at the real captives.

They were all still doped, sitting against the wall with their heads on their chests. Bemoaning the fact that it had all been for nothing, I quickly untied myself then went into the kitchen and put on the kettle.

The problem here was that I couldn't very well peek into the room at intervals to see if they were awake, because Harriet at least would be sure to recognise me even in disguise. So while I was working out the solution to this I lit up a handrolled and wet the tea.

It was at this point that I noticed the paper carrier bag hanging on the pantry door. Using a bread knife, I cut eyes in the bag, put it over my head then peeped into the spare room. They seemed to be more slumped over than ever, and I wondered what exactly Eddie was giving those people. It would be one of my trickiest situations ever if I wound up with three stiffs in my spare room. I had been in the *News of the World* before over some trifle, but they'd really dig up the dirt on that.

I went back into the kitchen and I was so worried about the entire set-up that I could hardly finish my tea. So I put on the bag again and wrapped a white sheet around me in case Harriet would wake up and recognise my suit.

In fact, it was a good precaution because when I stepped in all three of them were gazing at me with about the same degree of horror. I said to the tall heavy,

'The Imperial Priestess Eddie, who is our leader and who has made a zombie out of Barney Huggins, has no further use for him because he was using his subconscious to help you escape.'

I started to slow march around the room making large doodles in the air with my hand, and by the second circuit I had a nice little chant going.

'**O mea culpa quid pro quo in flagrante delicto O yea.**' I always knew my Latin phrases would come in handy sometime. '**O mea culpa quid pro quo in flagrante delicto O yea . . .**'

Now this was alright, but the trouble with chants is that you can get carried away, especially when they're echoing inside a carrier bag. It must have been the tenth or twelfth circuit when I started to hypnotise myself. In fact the next thing I knew I was passing through a crowd, which was melting smilingly before me, on the Lavender Hill.

'They showed some loonies like that on the telly,

60

only these ones preferred buckets.'

'Naw, he's from one of those Hindustani cults. Dint you hear him talkin' in foreign?'

'Wor? Wiv a Tesco bag on 'is 'ead?'

Well, I knew there was no point in making a spectacle of myself at this important stage of the game, so I brushed bruskly through the crowd and rushed up an alley where I stuffed my sheet and bag into a dustbin.

The pubs were now open so I strolled down to the Bunch of Grapes and had a quick pint while I pondered what had gone wrong. The only fault with my plan was that neither of the kidnappers — Eddie or the 'hooded man' — would be present after I had released us all. That might look suspicious. We needed somebody in the apartments who we could descend upon after we broke out of the spare room. We needed a fall-guy.

I said, 'Drink up, Petesy. I've got an interesting job for you.'

Petesy continued to stare at his army surplus boots. He was still in a huff over that Manley business.

'I'm not fussy about working for you anymore, Mr. 'Uggins. The only time you ever paid me properly was when you was passing those dud fivers. I should 'ave known better.'

'Don't worry,' I said, 'those days are over. How does ten quid sound?'

'Must be dangerous if you're paying that.'

'Not at all. I'm playing a joke on Harriet.'

Petesy's expression said that was dangerous enough, but after I'd bought him a scotch and another pint he started to feel better about the whole set-up.

On the way back I got the sheet and bag out of the dustbin, then I plied Petesy with three more whiskies and told him to dress up in the bedroom.

'Don't forget,' I told him. 'Don't come out until you hear us coming out of the spare room.'

'I wish you'd got a cleaner bag, Mr. 'Uggins.'

'Go on, get in there,' I said, pushing him into the bedroom. Then I tied myself up again.

I think my performance was better the second time around. I rolled and wrestled and gagged like a maniac. After I got tired of that, I lay still for a while, then I made a show of discovering how to untie my ropes.

I loosened Harriet's legs first, gave them a good massage and walked her slowly around the room. When I released her hands they shot up to pull out her gag, but I clamped a hand over her mouth and whispered,

'Not a peep. Eddie's henchmen are all over the place. Keep still while I untie these two.'

The wife seemed to have taken it very hard. There were long tear grooves down her make-up. She seemed almost grateful when I helped her to her feet. I felt almost sorry for her. But the tall heavy was still very upset. I could tell by his eyes that Petesy was going to earn his ten quid. I stood back sharpish when I untied the last knot on him.

'Get going,' I said and pushed Harriet into the living room. I waited until I heard a scream, all the while keeping an eye on the reanimating tall heavy, then I dashed out shouting, 'I'll save you, Harriet.'

By the staggers of the hooded figure groping his way towards the screaming Harriet, it was clear he had been at my whiskey when I was releasing the prisoners. So I gave him a couple of good clouts for that while I put on a desperate struggle which lasted for a good twenty seconds and ended with Petesy in the spare room.

We were on the street before I remembered the Stradivarius. 'Hold on,' I told Harriet. 'I've got to go back in there.'

She said not to go, but I was adamant. 'That violin is nearly priceless,' I explained, brushing aside her clinging hand.

As I reached down the Stradivarius from the wall, I could tell by the noise in the spare room that the wife had regained her voice and the tall heavy the use of his limbs.

I WAS GLAD SHE WAS WEARING
HER CORSET

Oddly enough I'd never been in Harriet's rooms before. When I saw them I knew why the mess in my place was the only thing she'd never complained about. They seemed alright at first sight, apart from the dust and scattering of used glasses. But when I started to notice on the floor the little designs made from nail clippings and clots of hair, I decided not to look closely at anything else. In fact I was tempted to take off my specs altogether.

'Yes, Harriet,' I said, putting a match to the mound of used tissues in the fireplace. 'I definitely will get you another fur coat.'

She splashed some whiskey into a couple of glasses and handed me one.

'You'd better. But I still can't believe that bitch was going to sacrifice me to this Dervish Devil you mentioned.'

'You would if you saw what I did. That hooded heavy wasn't chanting over you for nothing, you know. He meant business alright.'

She started to pace the room. 'Oh, I get excited just thinking of what I'll do when I get my hands on that whore.'

I said, 'You can have first go at her if you want, but you must let me handle this. We're playing with some of the most diabolical and craftiest mates in London, don't forget.'

'Yes, but I must do something now or I'll go crazy.'

'Not now,' I said. 'You're still in a bad way after your ordeal. Go to bed and I'll let you help me tomorrow.'

'Where are you going?'

'After Eddie,' I said. 'Where else?'

I finished off my drink and left her still pacing the floor. She was mad alright but I was pleased I had made Eddie the main target instead of me.

It was four o'clock and I was heading for Soho. On the way I stopped off at the bank to pick up the photo and negative.

Eddie was sitting on a long couch, holding her knees. She was wearing a blue slit skirt and a black frilly blouse. She seemed to be sad or thoughtful.

I said, 'Hand over the five hundred.'

Eddie just curled her lip.

I said, 'Come on, I've got it on me.'

Eddie snapped out of the dull blue glare. Suddenly all interest, she got to her feet and closed the door. She said,

'Give it to me.'

'Have you got the money?'

'Just about,' she said. 'Let me see it.'

'Alright,' I said, sliding the photo out of my pocket. 'But keep your hands off it.'

She nodded slowly. 'That's him okay.'

'In all his glory. See, I've even got the number of the house, and that face at the window is Lisa who ran the place. The last time I saw her she was covered in blood and had a knife in her hand. I never did find out how that case ended.'

'You were lucky with that shot, weren't you,' she said, going over to the couch. She pulled out a handbag from behind it and clicked it open.

'Not really,' I said. 'I spent two days snapping all movement in and out of that place, so I was bound to get something good.'

'Yes, I'm sure your client was very pleased with you too. Give me the photograph and the negative.'

As I counted the money she said, 'It's all there, less ninety quid for services rendered.'

I'd almost forgotten about that. I was just going to make a comment when the door opened to reveal a short nervous bloke wearing glasses.

Eddie said, 'Come in, this gentleman's just leaving.'

I said, 'I'd better tell you something first.'

'Not now. I'll talk to you later.'

'Just as you wish,' I said. I couldn't force her to hear about the tall heavy escaping. But she'd know better than to brush me off like that again. I banged the door behind me and stepped out into the narrow Soho street.

As I'd expected, I didn't have a dog's chance of getting out of there alive with Eddie's fur coat. Harriet definitely had to be mollified, so there was nothing for it but to pay good money for one down the market. Unless, of course, I was able to rent or borrow one.

Yes, that was it, and I knew just the place for it too. I hadn't been working for Big Max all those months for nothing. In fact this particular fence had his office just down the street from where I was.

Frankie handed me the coat and said, 'One week, that's all you've got. Savez?'

I savied beaucoup alright. Frankie's heavy used to work for the Krays. He was thrown out of that firm because he was too rough. I said,

'You bet, Frankie, and there won't be a mark on it.'

Frankie just gave me a mean smile which said volumes about the consequences of losing or even dirtying the coat. So I said thanks again and got out before he changed his mind.

On the way back on the tube I had a few qualms about leaving Eddie in a tight spot. But when I opened the door to Harriet's rooms I realised I should have been more anxious about myself and poor old Harriet.

I said to the tall heavy, who was holding Harriet by the neck with one hand and pointing a revolver at me with the other,

'Hold on a minute there. That woman is bad enough with her nerves as it is, without you coming in and choking her. In fact —'

'Shut up!' For a moment I thought the tall heavy was going to scream or cry, and knowing enough to realise you don't annoy an hysterical man holding a gun, I decided to do as he said and shut up.

'Where's Eddie?'

I had a feeling this was going to be a tricky round of questioning. 'As far as I know,' I said after a moment, 'she's still operating out of my apartments. I would have thought you knew that.'

Releasing Harriet, he lurched towards me, waving me away from the door with his gun. 'Get over there,' he snarled, pushing me towards Harriet, who looked to be on the brink of either breaking down or going berserk.

I didn't like it when he said, 'Your dumb act didn't fool me, Huggins. Only a stupid bitch like her would fall for that. And that bloke I clobbered was begging to tell me how you set him up. You think I didn't know all along you were working for Eddie?'

I particularly didn't like it when he added, 'Which puts you right in it, mate, because the Captain's put a contract out on her.'

'Eddie?'

'Yeah, she shopped him after he slashed her for whoring around. The mug he found her with got cut up in a different place.'

I managed to say, 'How was I to know that? I thought I was helping the Captain. I mean, she said you had shopped him —'

'It's too late, fella. You've gone too far this time. The firm's under pressure and we need to make one or two examples.'

I swallowed hard. 'You mean?'

'That's right, Muggins. It's the high jump for you.'

Harriet said, 'Let me out of here! I don't want to watch. I promise I won't say anything.'

She tried to fall to her knees but I threw my arm around her neck and held her in front of me. I was glad she was wearing her corset.

It was a grim few moments as we slowly advanced on the gunman, my body tensing for the crucial flurry of action.

Then he gave a severe smile and said, 'I'm going to give you a chance, Huggins.'

68

'What do you mean?' I said, stopping about three feet from him.

'It's about that rap you beat. Word's just come to me you fixed the judge. Say how you done it and you're safe from this shooter.'

'What am I not safe from?'

'You and me have a score to settle. Personal, like.'

'How will that be settled?'

'Ask that joker in the sheet. By the look of your mug you've had worse.'

'Alright,' I said, not sure that I wasn't moving into a tighter spot than before. 'I had a photo that proved he went to a callgirl who specialised in some pretty weird stuff. I think he was more worried about his wife seeing it than anyone else.'

'That sounds good. Where is it now?'

'Eddie's got it.'

'Eddie?'

I started to tense up again. 'Yes, she said she needed it to save the Captain. She's got the negative too.'

For a good ten seconds he fixed me with an awful gaze. I started to watch his trigger finger then switched to the tic under his left eye. I don't know what Harriet was looking at, she just sagged against my arm, making deep rumbling noises in her throat.

'You idiot!' he roared, stepping forward with a vicious backhander which caught Harriet on the nose. 'This was Eddie's plan all the time. She wants the Captain to go down for this one. Can't you see that?'

Well, I could see it now alright. But I think he was being very unfair expecting me to have caught it on at the start. I said,

'She's got this place in Soho. If we're quick we might catch her.'

He gave me another withering look and for a moment I thought he was going to hit Harriet again.

'Fat chance of that. She'll not stick around now she has the snap. We'll check it out anyway, but I've a feeling you've a mighty big job on your hands, Huggins.'

'What do you mean?' I said.

'I mean if she's not there you'll be responsible for finding her.'

Harriet was bleeding over my sleeve so I let her slump to the floor. I said,

'Are you serious? She could be anywhere. She could be in Manchester or Scotland by now. She might even be leaving the country.'

'That's your problem,' the tall heavy snapped. 'You're supposed to be the detective, not me.'

I said, 'I'm not good at missing persons. Look, a client asked me to deal with his wife but I looked everywhere and still couldn't find her. And she's not even missing. I couldn't even find her in her own house.'

But he wasn't impressed. 'The stakes are high enough,' he said, 'so you'll track her down alright. Come on, let's go.'

At the door he said, 'Tell that tart I was aiming for you.'

'Don't worry about it,' I told him as he pushed me out into the corridor.

IT'S ALMOST IMPOSSIBLE TO GET A WOMAN OUT OF A HOUSE QUICKLY

As I'd expected, Eddie had flown the coop.

The tall heavy painted scenes of horrible torture while he tightened the knot of my tie. Then he socked me in the solar plexus, following up with a hook to the nose as I doubled over. I didn't know if this counted as part of his personal score or not, but I only let him do it because I felt guilty about taking him prisoner.

I spent the night getting drunk in my apartments. It was a good job for Eddie she didn't show up because I was feeling very aggrieved about the whole set-up. It was high time, I decided, to do some hitting back in this case.

The next morning at Harriet's rooms when she tried to brain me with an empty sherry bottle I just grabbed her arm and twisted it behind her back.

'It's a pity,' I said, forcing her face against the wall, 'you weren't so brave last night instead of cowering about with your head between your legs. At least I was doing something about the situation.'

I let her go and she slewed round, snarling and snapping and clawing at my face. I raced into her unmade bedroom and as she stormed in I threw the fur coat over her, holding her down until she stopped jerking and struggling.

I said, 'You and me are finished, Harriet. I'm fed up to the teeth with you. You're the rottenest and most miserable girlfriend I've ever had. All you do is drink the piece out and pick rows with everybody. In other words you're a bastard.

'And,' I added, angrily sweeping the coat off her, 'I'm taking this fur with me too.'

Well, I wasn't halfways to the door before she started into a whole carry-on about being sorry and how she was going to do herself in. So I went back and told her she had another chance, which was a relief to me too since I badly needed a base in order to continue the search for Eddie.

In fact, as I said to Harriet, there wasn't a minute to lose. But it's almost impossible to get a woman out of a house quickly, and it was nearly ninety minutes later before we were outside Eddie's place in Soho.

'I'm looking for a lead,' I told Harriet as she stared at Eddie's Gents Tailoring sign. I said, 'That needlework came as a surprise to me too.'

Harriet started, 'Don't be — ' Then she remembered herself and said, 'Barney, this means she duffs up men for money. Didn't you know that?'

'Of course I did. Needlework's a sophisticated way of

saying that. Just like being on Ugandan Business means having a screw.'

I led the way in. The door was open because I'd kicked it in the night before. After we'd searched a bit it became clear that Harriet didn't understand what looking for a lead meant. She said,

'You better tell me what a lead looks like.'

I said, 'We won't know until we find it. It could be anything. I once found —' Then I broke off as a hulking constable filled the doorway.

While he and Harriet exchanged steely glints, I took out my silver cigarette case and fired up a handrolled.

'Still raining out there?' I asked casually.

He said, 'I've been watching you, miss, for several days. Aren't you aware of the new law banning this kind of solicitation?'

Harriet had to laugh. 'It's Eddie you're looking for, copper. You're mixing us up because she wears a coat like this. I've never been here before. He can tell you.'

It was now my turn to say something. Harriet looked at me expectantly, waiting in her simple way for me to back her up. Normally I would have, but in this case I didn't know if the constable had noticed the broken lock. With only a couple of weeks to the Captain's trial, getting pulled in now could be disastrous.

'Well, tell him, Barney.'

It was a tricky situation alright, particularly since Harriet had drawn his attention to Frankie's coat. His eyes were definitely on it as he stood in the doorway, blocking my chance of an easy escape.

I said, 'Sorry, Eddie. It's a fair cop.'

Harriet's face was a picture as the constable strutted towards her, pulling out his notebook. Her mouth opened speechlessly and her adams apple

73

wobbled like a turkey's. I just shrugged and handed the constable my card.

B.H. HUGGINS

DISCRETE INVESTIGATIONS

I said, 'Don't get the wrong idea. I can spell alright, but what happened was that this printer put the T and E back to front by mistake. Naturally, I refused to pay —'

'Yes, sir, I can see what you mean. Just give me a few details and then you can leave.'

'Well, I came in to get some buttons sewn on but as soon as I saw Eddie here I knew there was something fishy going on —'

I broke off at this point because Harriet had just unleashed a wild farmhouse right that was caught in mid-air by the constable. The last thing I saw as I backed out of the door was the helmetless copper twisting Harriet's arm behind her back.

That's Harriet all over, I thought, looking for a pub. She always has to make things worse for herself. I mean, she must have known I had a good reason for handing her over. The way she was gaping at me you'd have thought I did it out of badness or because I'd set the whole thing up.

But it was funny how my cases always seemed to throw up a lot of casualties. That business with Lisa and the dud money was more ferocious at times than Korea. Even my client disappeared halfways through that one. I think he was afraid I'd discovered too much.

This case was different in that way. I was still looking for my first breakthrough. I was also still looking for somebody who would pay for all this. In both

74

senses. The tall heavy seemed to think I'd nothing better to do than rush to the Captain's aid whenever he got in a police jam.

But as I entered the pub, I had a feeling he'd be getting a sharp reminder it wasn't as simple as that. There was more to this case than met the eye and I'd an idea that Eddie, for all her cunning, wasn't the brains behind the plot to screw the Captain.

In fact, after I'd downed a couple of quick whiskies, I had a fancy that the fate of the Captain was small potatoes compared to the real issue at stake here. It was just a matter of seeing through the smokescreen and finding out what it was.

THE WHOLE THING FIZZLED OUT
LIKE A DAMP PUNCTURE

I didn't see much point in tramping around in the rain without a plan, so I stayed in the pub until half two. By that time I had decided that it was almost certain Eddie was still in town. First, she had no money. Second, she couldn't go on the run without money. Third, London was her best bet for earning some. Fourth, I couldn't assume she wanted to go on the run.

In other words, Eddie was either following her old trade or preparing for the second phase of her plan. Possibly she was doing both. But streetwalkers are like coppers and taxi drivers. You can never see one when you need them. So I decided to start at the first massage parlour or escort agency and broaden my search from there.

The rain had stopped, but the pavement was so slick I had a little trouble at first keeping my balance. But I made it to the Yellow Table Massage alright and said to the girl behind the desk,

'You got anybody with a scar here?'

'A scar?' she drawled, leaving her mouth open after she'd wrung as much distaste as she could out of the word. Her teeth were yellow and narrow like a rat's.

'That's right,' I said. 'One that's long and white and raised. You can't miss it.'

She sighed and shook her head. She brought her hand up and looked down at her nails as if she was going to nibble them.

'What's that mean?' I said, leaning over the desk. 'No? Don't know? Or don't care? Don't you like working here?'

'I did until today,' she snapped, rising from her chair. 'You'd better talk to the manager.'

After she'd gone out through a door to the right, I sat down on the desk and lit up one of her cigarettes. It was one of those milds that burn to the filter while you're still heaving for the first drag.

I expected the manager to be a hard geezer, but this one was round and soft all over. She swayed in wearing a cute black number and bounced over to the desk, parting her glossy red lips in a golden smile.

'The girl's only new,' she said, making a nice little flourish with her treble chins. 'But she'll understand what men like soon enough. Just give me twenty quid, ducks, and you can go down and see the lady with the scar.'

I said, 'Is it okay to just talk to her for a moment? I don't want a massage.'

Her smile faded. 'Not here you don't. We don't allow

77

time-wasters in here.'

I showed her my card. 'Look, this is official business I'm on.'

'Huh! Official my arse. You're private and that's nowhere in my book. Come on, pay up or get out.'

I said, 'Okay,' and gave her two tenners.

She said, 'Room four, down the corridor. There's a star on the door. Don't make any more trouble.'

I went down the corridor. The door was black with a yellow star. There was a metal 4 at the top and below that a stick-on plastic 4. I thought, they must take the customers for right morons here. I went inside and closed the door. There was a yellow plastic cover over the weak bulb, giving the tiny room a yellow glow.

There was the plonk of chunky heels in the corridor, then the door opened slowly to reveal a face that wasn't Eddie's.

She said, 'You'd better get undressed.'

She came in and started to unbutton her blouse. It had three buttons. They looked polished and the top one was hanging by a thread.

I said, 'Sure you've got the right room?'

'Of course I'm sure. This is my room. Doesn't bother me if you don't want a rub. The manager said you were a time-waster.'

I said, 'The one I wanted had a scar.'

She snapped open her skirt. 'You're looking at it, mate,' she said, showing me her appendix scar. 'That's what you asked for, isn't it?'

'Not really,' I said. 'But I've seen worse.'

She stepped out of her skirt. Her white cotton briefs had a yellow lustre, and even though there was a small electric fire in the room I could see goose pimples on her bare legs.

She said, 'What is it you want?'

I took off my trousers and lay on the bench. 'Seeing that I'm here, I may as well get my money's worth. A bit of relief, that's all.'

'Another five, then,' she said, standing with hands on hips, still wearing her bra.

What the hell, I thought, and reached over for my trousers. I counted out five singles then lay back on the bench.

She started off by running her hands down my legs, which by now had their own goose pimples. She wasn't applying much elbow grease, but the calluses on her hands were doing in a few of the pimples.

I ran my hand up her leg to her buttocks. She slapped it away.

'No touching,' she said. 'That's extra.'

I said, 'What about some oil, then? Or is that extra too?'

She turned and jerked a bottle of baby oil from a small table. After she'd splashed it over me several times there was more grease on my chest than on Harriet's kitchen wall. There were small pools in the dents and a stream ran down from my stomach onto my thigh. With two sweeps of her hand she smeared it over my legs and crotch.

She was making a small effort now. It couldn't have been easy for her trying to finish me off in thirty seconds while she kept losing her grip. Then she stopped at exactly the wrong moment and the whole thing fizzled out like a damp puncture.

After handing me a couple of tissues she climbed into her skirt and went out, buttoning her blouse. I used the rest of the box of tissues to clean myself up, then I got dressed and went out in search of a wash basin.

As I'd expected, there was no hot water and no soap, but I was able to wash my hands with the soapy scum on the ledge between the taps.

I was in a bad mood as I left the Yellow Table Massage and I certainly had no time for that snoop Manley, who was waiting outside in his muffler and soft hat and puffing on a large curved pipe like he was ruddy Sherlock Holmes. I said sharply,

'Didn't I teach you before not to follow me? Didn't I?'

He just stood there, looking levelly at me, and sending little puffs of smoke out of the corner of his mouth. Finally, just as I was about to belt him one, he said,

'I don't think you're in a position to threaten anybody.'

'What do you mean?' I asked.

'It's not complicated. Your wife has merely filed a complaint with the police that you assaulted and kidnapped her. Quite routine stuff for you, I imagine.'

'Well, you imagine wrong,' I snapped. 'If the old bag could bring herself to tell the truth she'd have to admit it was me who released her. I was a prisoner of Eddie too, you know. In fact —'

'Eddie?' he said. 'Who's he?'

'She's a tart.'

'Was she the woman you were following that morning?'

'That's right. She's the key to this entire case. I'm having a hell of a time trying to find her.'

'Oh yes. I was a little inquisitive about her relationship with you, so one evening I followed her back to her rooms —'

'To my apartments, you mean?'

80

He shook his head. 'I don't mean that at all.' He smiled and ran the mouthpiece of his pipe along his lips.

I said, 'That's very interesting, but I've already checked her rooms. Those are the ones at . . .?'

But he wasn't being drawn. 'If you've already checked I can't help you,' he said and started to walk away.

'Wait. What do you want for it?'

He turned. 'Your co-operation. Starting with the return of the Stradivarius to its rightful owner.'

I had a feeling he was going to say that. I said, 'Alright. Are you still at the same hotel?'

'Yes.'

'I'll bring it round at seven. That okay?'

'Make sure you come alone. A man in your position would be ill advised to attempt any funny stuff.'

'Well, this is it,' I said. 'I'm on a very sticky wicket at the moment. You could even turn me in if you wanted to.'

'Precisely,' he said and walked off, merging smoothly with the crowd.

I stepped into the doorway of the bookshop we'd been standing outside and lit a cigarette. I stood there for a long five minutes, smoking thoughtfully and sizing up the situation. Then I went down to the phone box on the corner and put through a short message to the tall heavy.

THE TALL HEAVY COULD HARDLY BELIEVE HIS LUCK

It was opening time at the Bunch of Grapes. I set up two pints of best bitter and said,

'Look, Petesy, when I was in Korea the officers lied to us all the time. "Barney," they would say, "we're sending you and the boys on furlough. Quiet little retreat in the country just north of here. Don't forget your rifles." The next thing we knew we were being dropped along the Chinese border with half a million little Commies disguised as trees waiting for us.

'So you see, Petesy, detective work is like war. The ordinary five-eighths have to be kept in the dark sometimes, because if the chap who's running the show clued them in to what's really happening they might start to think for themselves, and then the whole campaign would turn into a shambles. Now do you understand?'

Petesy remained hunched up in his raincoat and beret, the pint of beer still untouched. 'I don't care. You've still got to be able to trust people.'

'Precisely. You've also got to know people. If you had used your loaf you would have known I don't pay out ten quid just to play a joke on Harriet. Isn't that another way of looking at it?'

'You mean I've only meself to blame?'

'Not exactly,' I said, 'but it'll teach you to be more careful in future. I don't like anybody working for me who's not careful.'

I pulled out my wallet. 'And don't think I don't look after my men. Here's ten quid for your trouble.'

'And,' I added, putting down two more fivers, 'here's another ten quid for a very easy bit of following that I want done tonight. No danger involved in this one at all.'

He looked at me sideways. 'I don't get the ten nicker for me trouble if I don't take the job?'

'Course not. How can I pay you that if you're not working for me anymore?'

'Alright, Mr. 'Uggins,' he said, reaching for his pint. 'You're on.'

'Good man.' I finished off my own pint. 'Come on, get that down you. We've got to be in Paddington in half an hour.'

Petesy liked the chance to show his prowess at chug-a-lugging beer, and it wasn't his fault, but the tube's, that it was 7:15 before we were outside Manley's hotel.

I said, 'Don't be getting nervous now, Petesy, but the bloke who's up with the pansy detective is the same one who duffed you up at my apartments.'

83

He sank further into his raincoat. 'Oh gawd blimey.'

'Yes, and when he comes out he'll be going with me to Eddie's place. You follow us from there to wherever we're going. If he pulls a stunt on me, just play it by ear. I'm not expecting you to rush in and get another thumping. But if Eddie comes out first you'll know something has gone wrong, so you'll tag along behind her. Got that? Good. Now make yourself scarce.'

Petesy shuffled away and I stepped back into the darkness of an alley. By the time I'd smoked two handrolleds I was getting fed up standing there in the cold and damp. I couldn't see why Manley hadn't told him straight off where Eddie was holed up, instead of making the tall heavy go through the rigmarole of beating it out of him. He'd definitely been reading too much Philip Marlowe, I thought.

Finally the tall heavy came out. He looked quickly to both sides then started off down the street. Not so fast, buster, I thought, and ran across the road after him.

'Any luck?' I said.

He kept walking. 'Yeah. About a mile from here. We'll take a cab.'

'Was he difficult?'

'Don't ask,' he said tightly, which perhaps said it all.

It was lucky for Petesy we couldn't see a cab, so we caught a bus which brought us onto the Bayswater Rd.

When I saw the building I knew that Eddie really was short of money. Two of the windows had cardboard instead of glass. The front door was banging in the wind. One of the steps crumbled as I stepped on it. A sodden paperback lay in the hall.

I picked it up then continued after the tall heavy, who was taking the unlit stairs two at a time. There was no sign of him when I reached the first landing, just the

84

dull thump of his steps above.

I trudged up to the next storey and listened. All was quiet except for the wind, the tapping of the front door and the faded notes of a clarinet from a room somewhere below.

A door stood ajar, emitting a shaft of harsh yellow light. I moved silently towards it. I stood there, listening, being very quiet, for about twenty seconds. Then I pushed open the door and walked into it again.

Eddie said, 'Come on in. I didn't want to start without you.'

I said to the tall heavy, 'You bloody fool!'

Eddie said, 'No fun without Punch, I always say.'

I said, 'It was a good trick of mine to lure him here. Wasn't it, Eddie?'

She said, 'Either come in or I'll shoot you where you stand.'

I was standing wrong-footed for a break into the hall, so I just shrugged and went over and stood by the tall heavy. Eddie was leaning against the wall, directing my movements with the gun. She pointed it cleanly, easily, like it was one of her fingers. She said,

'You boys haven't given me much choice. That's a pity.'

I said, 'What do you mean?'

She gave a slight smile. Her eyes were wide, mocking. 'A detective to the end. Still asking questions when you already know the answer —'

'Look, Eddie,' the tall heavy broke in, 'it's still not too late. We can make a deal. Five grand for the photo. How's that sound?'

I said, 'Wait a minute. I was the one who took that photo and I only got five hundred for it.'

'That's enough,' Eddie snapped. 'No more stalling.

Put your hands on your heads and kneel down. Come on, get them up.'

Something had been nagging me about Eddie's gun, and as I raised my arms I suddenly realised what it was. It was a Colt 45 automatic — the exact same model as I kept under the socks in my bedroom drawer. I hadn't looked at it for some time but it was a cinch Eddie had found it when she searched my rooms. She probably realised it was only a replica, but if she hadn't checked the magazine there was a possibility she thought it genuine. There was also the possibility this wasn't the same gun at all. There was only one way to find out.

I said to the tall heavy, 'Relax, pal, Eddie's only playing a trick on us. That gun's an imitation 45 she took from my bedroom.' I forced a chuckle. 'Nice try, Eddie. You had us going there for a little while.'

The tall heavy could hardly believe his luck. As he turned to look at me his gaze was a mixture of hope and doubt. When I gave him a reassuring little nod he smiled grimly and reached into his coat. I don't think Eddie was trying to be sporting, but she did wait until his revolver was out before she shot him.

I didn't see how he fell. I was too busy hitting the deck and rolling behind an armchair. But those 45's pack quite a punch and I wouldn't have been surprised if he'd been lifted clean off his feet and spun round a few times.

It must have been something like that, because when I did finally peek out he was lying with his arms outstretched towards me. His revolver was sitting about two feet past his fingertips.

I didn't know where Eddie was, so I got to my knees and started to push the armchair towards the revolver. It didn't want to move at first, being very heavy and stuck to the carpet, but it couldn't resist my desperate pushing and within thirty seconds my fingers were closing around the cold revolver.

I called, 'You shouldn't have done that, Eddie. The cops will be here any minute. Get out while you can.'

There was no answer so I made a dash for the other armchair and scrutinised the room from there. It seemed to be empty, so I made another dash for the door and went down the stairs a lot quicker than I'd come up them. Which was just as well since I barely made it to the corner before a cop car came screeching to a halt in front of the building.

I HOPE YOU KNOW WHAT YOU'RE DOING, MR. 'UGGINS

I took the tube back to the Bunch of Grapes. I sat in the end snug drinking rum and wondering where Petesy was. About half eight Emily poked her head in and said there was a phone call for me.

It was Petesy. He said, 'I'm on the Fulham Palace Rd. She's gone into Buffer Bartley's gaff.'

This was bad news since the Buffer was a foremost G.B.H. specialist. I said, 'I'll be right down. Where'll I meet you?'

'I'm at the corner with the Fulham Rd. I can see the 'ouse from 'ere.'

'Alright,' I said, 'wait there till I come.'

I caught a bus into Fulham. By the time I arrived I had worked out a plan.

I said, 'Good work, Petesy. Any problems?'

'Nah, she was in too much of an 'urry to take any precautions.'

He didn't look at all worried, so it seemed that if he had heard the shot he hadn't recognised it as one or connected it with Eddie. I didn't think it was a good idea to mention she had a gun. I said,

'Here's thirty quid. Round up about ten of your mates and get them down here pronto.'

'What's the idea, Mr. 'Uggins?'

'The idea, Petesy, is that you get a bonus if you do as I say without any questions. Alright?'

He looked doubtful, so I said, 'A ten quid bonus plus what you make out of the deal. I mean, you don't have to give them thirty if they'll come for less. Get the idea?'

'Alright, but I don't like it.'

'Don't forget,' I added as he shuffled away, 'you don't have to mention anything about the Buffer.'

I set off to recce the target. It was a two-storey house at the end of the street. The garden was weeds and the brickwork was cracked above the door. A light shone in the living room window. A narrow lane led to the back of the house, where a 74 Escort was parked beside a tree.

I returned to the phone box and stepped in out of the light rain. It was a good plan, I thought, to employ shock-troops. Even if they didn't overwhelm Eddie and her henchmen on the first wave, I would be coming in after them with my revolver to clean up. It couldn't fail.

I waited for Petesy for over ninety minutes. Every now and then somebody would come to phone and they'd be giving me dirty looks as they stepped into the smoke-filled booth. Then Petesy arrived, tapping on the glass, and I went outside to see what he'd rounded up for me.

'Line the men up out of sight of the house,' I said,

handing him a fiver. 'Then go off and get two or three bottles of cheap sherry. You'll know what to get.'

'Listen here, men,' I said after Petesy had done his best to form them up. 'You can count yourselves lucky Petesy has picked you for this bit of fun.'

'Fun?' said a small bloke in a bush hat.

'Yes, that's what I said. I said fun. What's more — and this is probably what some of youse can't believe — you're going to get paid for it. Yes, paid for it.'

'We want our money first,' said the small troublemaker.

'There's always one of them, isn't there?' I said to the others. 'There's always a big mouth who wants to spoil things for the rest.'

There was a murmur of agreement.

'Belt up, Cecil.'

'Yeah, keep your trap shut, mate.'

'That's the idea,' I said, wondering if I should give Cecil a couple of backhanders to set an example. 'And to make extra sure we do have a good time, our friend Petesy is at this very moment on his way back here with an armful of booze!'

Holding my hands up to quell the shouts of approval, I added, 'But before we have our booze we're going to start the fun rolling by spreading out and looking quietly — I said, looking quietly — for something that can be used as a battering ram. Now off youse go. Be back here in ten minutes.'

As I watched the shock-troops tramp off I had to admit that Petesy had outdone himself this time. Even Lovecraft couldn't have thought up a more horrible fright than to have this lot come howling through the door.

It was a pity, I thought, that Cecil was too small to

be in the spearhead of the attack. Even with his bush hat he wouldn't have been over five feet. So I decided on the fat man, who was wearing a luminous yellow jacket like the lollipop men have, and a tall bag of bones in a dinner jacket that came halfway up his arms.

Behind them would come the three tramps. The first of which had only one ear, the second was wearing a woman's coat, and the third seemed unable to stop nodding his head.

Then the small sizes. Cecil and an even shorter individual with red golliwog hair.

Finishing up with the dregs. An old timer with a white beard from his eyes to his belt, and a creature in a long black coat and beret who bore a strange resemblance to Petesy's aunt.

And what a load of rubbish they brought back as battering rams. Two tyres, a dustbin and a crate of milk bottles.

I said, 'Good work, men. Now we'll have a drink. Petesy, pass out the booze. One bottle between three.'

Time was running short, but I had no need to tell these fellows to get it down them. They were lapping it up like nobody's business. I said to Petesy,

'You better get in there quick if you want a slug.'

He gave me a sour look and I said, 'I don't blame you.'

Cecil said, 'I don't call that a proper drink.'

'Don't worrry, men,' I told them, 'that's only the first taste. Further rewards lie in that house over there.' I pointed out the target.

'But,' I warned them, 'there are people in that house who want to hog all the booze to themselves, even though it is rightfully ours. What do you say about that, men?'

There was a chorus of boo's and murmured threats. Even Cecil was now on my side. I added,

'And I ask you. Are we as free men of England going to let them get away with that?'

Well, it was all I could do to stop them rushing the place there and then. They growled and complained and shouted obscenities at the house. Cecil practised his charge by running across the street and back again, and the fat man started to sing 'Land of Hope and Glory'.

Petesy touched my elbow. 'I hope you know what you're doing Mr. 'Uggins.'

'Don't worry,' I said. 'Organised chaos is one of the best tough tactics there is. You never know what you're going to find.'

I said, 'Right, men. The time has come,' and with a wave of my hand I led them across the street and down the lane to the back of the unsuspecting house.

'We're in luck,' I said to the fat man. 'Get that ladder and lay it beside the back door.'

While he was doing that I busied myself with the Escort. It was the work of mere moments to cross a wire or two and start the engine.

'Now remember,' I told them after they'd taken up their positions on the ladder, about ten yards from the door. 'Once you're inside, plenty of screaming and don't stop for anybody.

'On the count of three. One ... two ... **Wait for it, Cecil** ... Three!'

On the word of command the shock-troops set off with great determination for the door. If the fat man, Cecil, the old-timer and two of the tramps hadn't fallen over, they would probably have made it too.

HER LONG NAILS
DIGGING INTO MY SCALP

Not that I cared how big a mess they made of it. I needed all the diversion I could get. I was up against Buffer Bartley and Eddie's Colt 45, and time was running out.

I said to Cecil, 'You're in charge, mate. Get them lined up for another bash.' Then I got into the Escort and backed down the lane to the front of the house.

My plan was working quicker than I thought. Eddie was already making tracks. In fact, she was almost falling over herself to get away from the assault force, whose shouts of triumph could now be heard above the sound of the motor.

But there was no way she was going to escape me this time. I'd been through too much to let that happen.

It wasn't just the photo anymore, it was something bigger and more vital that was driving me to subdue her. I could feel it in my gut.

Gunning the engine, I mounted the kerb and aimed the car at Eddie. There were no lamp-posts or parked cars, just a fur-clad figure scurrying to the corner. I was almost upon her before she looked round, gazed in terror for a long second, then threw herself into a garden.

Screeching to a halt, I jumped in after her and socked her on the chin. I grabbed her handbag, I bundled her into the car then drove off fast towards my apartments. Glancing in the sun-visor mirror, I found myself grinning like a wolf.

Eddie was only dazed, so I had to pull over and tie her hands behind her back.

She said, 'You do think them up, don't you?'

I shrugged. 'It was fast and bloodless and successful. What more do you want?'

In spite of her situation she had to agree. Our eyes met and I could see a new respect in her look. She said, 'Yes, it was probably the only way you could have taken me. You can be a cunning bastard when you feel like it.'

'I have my moments. How did the Buffer take it?'

'I was there on my own. I hope he doesn't blame me when he gets back.'

'That's the least of your worries,' I said, pulling up outside my apartments. 'Make any trouble going in here and you'll wish you hadn't. Right?'

'I'll be good, Barney,' she said with a smile that suggested I was wasting my time. 'After all, you have me completely in your power. Don't you?'

'You better believe it,' I said, and pushed her down the steps.

The place was a shambles. The T.V. screen was kicked in and my paintings and musical instruments were lying smashed on the floor.

'Get the whiskey from the kitchen,' I told Eddie, then knelt down and ran my fingers over a mandolin-banjo I'd never play again.

'You're trouble, you know that?' I said when she came back. I put the bottle to my mouth and glared at her as the whiskey trickled down my chin.

I lit a cigarette and stood there for a few moments wondering whether it was Petesy or the tall heavy. Then I opened her handbag and tipped the contents onto the floor.

A Colt 45, a knuckleduster, keys, a pack of Players, matches, a compact, lipstick and a comb. There was no photo or negative. I said,

'Turn out the pockets of your coat.'

There was nothing there either. 'Alright, take the rest off.'

She just smiled and pulled the silk scarf from her neck.

I didn't like it. I had been expecting some resistance, a confrontation in which I would wave the tall heavy's gun at her before roughing her up and ripping off her clothes while she screamed defiance. I said,

'I don't think you have the photo any more.'

'That's right,' she said through the jumper she was pulling over her head, 'I burned it yesterday.'

'Most people would keep something like that. It's useful to bargain with.'

She stepped out of her skirt. 'Maybe I don't need it. What do you think?'

As I felt her for the photo, I was thinking of what happened the last time she lured me into her trap. But

95

it's very difficult to steel yourself against temptation when you have to run your hands along a silk-covered crotch.

Yes, she'd finally splashed out on a new set of underwear. The purple briefs and bra stood out tightly with a lustre that was even more eyecatching than the silver zig-zag design on her grey stockings that were held up at mid-thigh by elasticated tops. I ran my fingers slowly over a long run behind the knee and thought of the stocking tearing as she dived into the garden.

She said, 'What are you going to do now?'

The cigarette was burning low in my mouth so I flicked it into the fireplace. I took a mouthful of whiskey, swallowing it slow in a warm stream that ran down the back of my throat. I took off my hat for no reason at all, looked inside it, then put it on again. I handed her the bottle. I said,

'I'm giving you to the Captain.'

'That's nice.' She took a short swig then brushed against me as she went over to my armchair and sat down, crossing her legs.

'I'm in a spot,' I said. 'I have to give him something.'

'Reach me my coat. It's chilly in here.'

'You've only yourself to blame,' I said, handing her the fur. 'If you'd levelled with me at the start, things might have been different.'

'They still could be.'

'What do you mean?'

'Well, the Captain's going down for a spell, his minder's just stopped a bullet, the rest of the firm are probably open to suggestion. Need I say more?'

'By the way,' I said, 'was that tall geezer only winged or what?'

She shrugged. 'I dunno. You were the last one out.'

96

'I didn't look. You were talking to Buffer Bartley about this take-over idea?'

'That's right. He's my new minder.'

Jesus, I thought. I said, 'He got off to a great start tonight, didn't he?'

'Yes, he'll be mad about that. He'll probably go around crippling people for the next few days in order to regain his reputation. Barney,' she smiled, 'be a dear and bring me my cigarettes. They're lying on the floor with the rest of my stuff.'

I put her things, minus the Colt 45, back in the handbag and gave it to her. 'So there's no point in handing you over to the Captain, then?'

'Not really.'

I lifted one of the cushions off the settee and took out some newspapers. After crumpling them up and placing them in the fireplace, I lifted my mandolin-banjo and set it on top. A sprinkle of whiskey, a match, then I sat on the floor and watched it blaze.

I was tired and a little drunk. I lit up a handrolled, my cigarette case shining as the flames flared and crackled. I had another drink, a long slug that I didn't enjoy and didn't need. I said,

'I'm not in a very happy position, am I?'

'Not overly so, no.' She reached for the bottle and took several small sips. 'Put that other banjo on the fire, then draw the curtains and put the light out. We don't need to advertise the fact that we're here.'

'You're right,' I said, getting up and going over to the switch. 'Particularly if the Buffer's around.'

'You wouldn't have to worry about him if you took the Captain's place.'

I had just drawn the curtains. I looked round. Her face, clearly visible in the firelight, was at once serious and strangely unsure.

'Just with you, you mean?'

'No. I need my own man to take over the firm. The Buffer's too thick, so that leaves you. You're tough, crafty, unscrupulous, experienced. All in all, you're my best bet.'

'In charge of the firm?'

'Yes, I can't put it any plainer.'

Still undecided, I sat down on the floor and gazed into the fire. I thought of the jam I was in, alone with no heavy mates, surrounded by enemies. I wondered what would become of me if I didn't go in with her. I wondered what would happen if I did. I looked at the burning banjo, now a smoking wreck with flames licking up from its belly, and it seemed to be an omen or a symbol of something. So I said,

'Yes, Eddie, I'm your man.'

'Oh Barney!' she exclaimed, and she was so happy she couldn't help grinning all over her face.

I said, 'The Captain's day is over,' and kissed her on the knee. I ran my tongue along the zig-zag design, feeling the changes in texture and the small imperfections. When I reached the stocking top she arched slightly and I lifted my head to permit the passing of the purple silk. I was pulling them over her high-heels when a loud knock came to the door, followed by three others.

I was kneeling perfectly still but she grasped my hair and whispered, 'Don't stop now, Barney. Just ignore it.'

As the knocking continued she brought me down onto her, holding me tightly, her long nails digging into my scalp. I stayed there for a long time, building up my energy after a tiring day, and it seemed ages before the knocker finally gave up and went away.

AT LEAST WE'D BE DEALING WITH
THE FLYING SQUAD

'You don't give up easy, do you?' I said, stepping into Harriet's rooms and surprising Manley as he was looking behind the overstuffed armchair near the kitchen.

It was the next morning. I could tell by the number of butts in the fireplace that Harriet had been back here. I went up to him and raised my hand. He flinched. I scratched my nose. I stared him straight in the eye. His cheeks were bruised and swollen, his lip was cut. I said,

'Looks like you can be persuaded to talk, after all.'

He just stood there, tensed up, glaring at me, and I smiled at the question he was obviously asking himself. Finally, deciding not to chance it, he unclenched his fists and said,

'It's only a matter of time before the police get you, Huggins. They know you were involved in the shooting last night.'

'You told them, I suppose?'

'Of course I told them,' he said sharply. 'I can't withhold information of that nature.'

'Is he a goner?'

'Don't you know?'

'No, I missed the news this morning.'

'I'm afraid,' he said, trying to step past me, 'that I can't discuss this with you any further.'

I tightened my grip on his arm. 'Why'd you come here? Where's Harriet?'

'I don't know.'

'It's the Strad you're after, isn't it?'

'I'm trying to recover the property of my client.'

'Don't give me that. That cow didn't know what a Strad looks like. You put her up to this, didn't you?'

'Don't be absurd.'

'We'll see who's being absurd,' I said, pushing him towards the window. The back seemed clear, an alley lined with dustbins, no cops in sight. There was no time to lose.

'Move yourself,' I said urgently, shoving him into the tiny bedroom. I opened the wardrobe and looked inside. Her clothes had gone, but she never seemed to have more than two suits anyway. At least she'd left the key.

'Don't make it hard for yourself,' I told him, 'just get in there quietly so I won't have to plug you.'

'You're only making it worse for yourself,' he said sternly, looking down at the Colt 45.

'Shut up,' I snapped. 'I've just about had enough of you.'

I pushed him in and he crouched down in the portable wardrobe, gazing up at me from under his soft hat as I closed the door and locked it.

I went down the fire escape and along the alley. I caught a bus to the underground station then took the tube to Holland Park, where I was meeting Eddie.

It wasn't raining, so I sat down on a bench outside the park. Firing up a handrolled, I began to consider the situation as it now stood, with particular emphasis on what Frankie would do if I failed to bring his fur coat back. Of course, he couldn't do much if I was inside being questioned about the shooting or the kidnapping charge. But that was hardly a solution to any of my problems. It still left the music to be faced at one time or another.

No, there was no two ways about it. It was a matter of either becoming a gang boss or being hounded and battered from pillar to post by Frankie's heavy, Manley and Buffer Bartley. Not to mention Harriet, the wife, the cops, and the tall heavy, if he hadn't got round to cashing in his chips yet.

But it was a cruel twist of fate, I thought, that I was being forced into a life of crime at this stage of my career. I mean, I was quite happy in my own way with what I was doing before Eddie came along. I had just started looking for McConkey's wife, a case that had great possibilities. There was the odd job from Big Max, which was interesting enough. And I was having a reasonably good time with Harriet, who was going through one of her mellower patches. Now I couldn't even go near the Bunch of Grapes without getting picked up. In fact, it was a wonder they hadn't nabbed me last night or this morning at Harriet's.

I was pondering these issues when a horn tooted and Eddie pulled up in the Escort. I jumped in and

Eddie zipped off towards Holland Park Ave., saying, 'Where's your banjo?'

'The Strad's gone,' I said, holding onto the dash as she created an extra lane to overtake a Mini. I let out my breath as the oncoming van rushed past with its horn blaring. 'Harriet must have taken it. I've just been through her rooms. She's got the fur as well.'

'Fur?'

'The one I got her to replace yours.'

'Really?' She gave a chuckle. We went through an amber light and I put on my seatbelt. 'You must be fond of her after all,' she said. 'Or else you want to keep her quiet.'

'Keep her quiet? You must be joking. No, it's only rented. I have to take it back soon.'

'Does she know that?'

'Not really.'

'It figures.' She jerked into third for another roaring overtake. There was a squeal of brakes from an approaching car, then a slight jolt and a shout as the back end swiped a man on a bicycle as we swung back into the lane.

I said, 'It's not smart to drive like that when you're on the run.'

'Who's on the run?'

'We are.' I told her what Manley had said about the shooting and the kidnapping.

She shook her head. 'Come on, Barney, smarten up. You're not going to win over the boys if you talk like that. Be confident, assert yourself, show them your gun, tell them how you put one over on the Buffer. That'll impress them alright. Tell them how easily you can take prisoners and how you tracked me down in a matter of hours. Look, I'll even let you say it was you who shot the Captain's minder. That's bound to get you some respect.'

'You're right,' I said, 'you can't graduate to the Big Time if you don't think positive. Why even Shakespeare said something like that in one of his heavy plays. Our doubts are traitors, he said.'

'That's the idea.'

Yes, I thought, taking out a handrolled and pushing in the dash lighter, she is right. I **had** underestimated myself. All these years, when the world was taking swipes at me, I hadn't believed in myself enough.

But now that I had a gang behind me it would be a whole new ball game. We'd clean up all round us, taking over rackets here and starting up rackets there, where there had been none before. And if we did come up against the cops, well, at least we'd be dealing with the Flying Squad instead of just Sgt. Mungo. And if the Buffer thought he should be the top banana instead of me, well, I'd just have to put my foot down and show them who's boss, including Eddie.

'Barney?'

'Yes.'

'We're almost there.'

'Good.'

'There's something I should tell you.'

I chuckled. 'I wish I had a quid for every time a woman's said that to me.'

'Well, the fact is, Buffer might be a little surprised to see you, that's all.'

'How come? Didn't you fill him in?'

'I tried to, but he kind of got the idea he was going to be my right hand man. The thing was, Barney, I had to promise him something to get him to help me. I was in a fix, you know I was.'

'That's terrific,' I said.

The traffic thickened and as we came to a halt outside Bayswater station, she smiled and reached over and grasped my thigh, trying to cheer me up. But I just shook my head and stared out of the window. I had a good mind to get out there and then and let her find some other fall-guy to be in charge of the gang.

HIS EYES WERE AS ROUND AND AS
BIG AS PENNIES

The door next to the Chinese restaurant was open. We went up a flight of stairs to another door which said UNCLE TEDS TOYS LTD. She opened it and said,

'Hi, Buffer. Nobody else arrived yet?'

'Doesn't look like it.'

He was sitting at a large wooden desk, filling his pipe and staring at me with obvious distaste.

'Don't I know you from somewhere?' he asked, flaring a match and holding it to the bowl.

'How do I know what you know?' I said, and smiled at the way his eyes flashed up at me.

Puffing at his pipe, he placed his forefinger inside the bowl to tamp down the tobacco, keeping it there as a cloud of smoke grew around him. He said to Eddie,

'What is this? Who's the smart geezer?'

'I forgot to tell you —'

'Save it, Eddie,' I said, stepping over to the front of the desk. I leant over and fixed him with a severe stare. 'What she forgot to tell you last night was that I was the one who was after her . . .'

His mouth dropped open then he started to smile like he couldn't believe his luck.

I banged the desk with my fist. 'Yes, that's right, me, Barney Huggins. And I don't take too kindly to lugs who put people up when I'm looking for them. In fact, I get very upset at them. And when I get upset . . .' I jerked out the Colt 45 '. . . I use this.'

He was a tough nut alright, but he still started when he saw the gun. His scarred eyes widened and he began to breathe a little heavier.

'See this gun?' I said. 'It's put paid to a lot of my problems, so make sure you're not one of them. Keep your nose clean, do what you're told, and you'll be okay. I might even forget about last night. You got that?'

He nodded. 'Whatever you say. I'm not arguing with a shooter.'

'That's alright then. Now get the hell out of here and round up those other buggers. Tell them to get their asses over here right now.'

Eddie stepped forward. 'Oh Barney, he doesn't know who they are. Maybe I'd better contact them myself.'

'I said he was to do that, didn't I?'

'But —'

'But nothing. Make him out a list. Come on, let's get things moving around here.'

She shrugged and made out the list. The Buffer

106

hauled his fifteen stone of hard muscle from behind the desk and slouched out, his eyes downturned from my steely gaze. Eddie said,

'God, you've got a nerve.'

I smiled. 'If I had any nerves in me I'd have been scared. But I had them all cut out before I went to Korea with the Commandos. Didn't want to go haywire on dangerous missions.'

She looked impressed. 'I never knew that.' Then she shook her head and grimaced. 'Go on with you. What a load of cobblers.'

'You never know,' I said. 'Look what they did with the Six Million Dollar Man.'

She stepped up and touched her moist lips against mine. 'He wasn't based on a real man, was he?'

I gave an inward smile and thought of my reconstructed nose, my steel jaw, the ear I'd had sewn back on and the plastic joint in my left elbow. The results of a car crash and numerous bouts of action. I said,

'I've often wondered about that myself. They probably could, you know. For a start, the Russians have developed these petrol-powered jumping boots. Now these could be —'

'Oh Barney, how can you talk about jumping boots when I'm standing this close to you? Am I losing you already?'

I didn't say anything. I just held her tight and kissed her. With one hand on her neck and the other gripping her backside, I kissed her so that she'd stay kissed for a long, long time.

Yes, I was already making plans for her future, and they didn't include B.H. Huggins. She was a hot property alright, but I wasn't about to let her pull the same stunt on me as she did the Captain.

'My, that was passionate,' she murmured and touched my chin with her tongue. 'I can't wait to get you home. I got so excited watching you make a little boy out of the Buffer.'

'So you liked my style?' I said, not mentioning the help I got from the three Valiums I'd taken before we left the car.

'Adored it. And what about mine?' She stepped back and held open her fur.

'You don't often see that nowadays,' I said, admiring her ruched costume of grey satin.

'No, they've been out of fashion for a long time. But this isn't all I wanted to show you. You're now going to see something quite remarkable.'

'Really?'

'Yes. But you can't see me doing it. Turn your back for a moment, it just takes a few seconds.'

It seemed harmless enough, so I stepped over to the window and peered through the venetian blinds at a line of overflowing dustbins in the back alley. There was about ten seconds of rustling noises from behind me, then she said,

'You can look now.'

When I turned round she was standing with her hands on her hips and a smug smile on her face, and it took me a couple of seconds to realise she was now wearing a plain dress of black satin instead of the ruched outfit she had on before.

'I don't believe this,' I said. 'You couldn't have changed that quickly.'

'How'd I do it then?' She took off her coat and turned on her toes like a model, letting me see the back was black satin too.

'Damned if I know. Is it reversible? Here, sit down

108

till I have a look at this.'

She sat down in the padded chair behind the desk. I was examining the inside of the dress, which was of course the grey ruche, and having another feel of the stockings with the zig-zag design, when the door opened. I was kneeling down behind the desk, so I couldn't see who it was, but I could hear a harsh voice saying,

'Well, stone me. What have we got here? Don't tell me her ladyship's decided to come see her old chums after all. What's the matter? Didn't you like being a working girl anymore?'

Eddie stiffened. I held onto her leg as she made a move to get up. She said to the bloke,

'Watch your mouth. Just hang about until the others arrive.'

'Including your new heavies, I suppose? These two hard geezers you've told us about?'

'You'll find out soon enough.'

'I've heard of Buffer Bartley alright, but not this other bloke who duffed up Les and then shot him. Sounds like a right mean bastard, don't he?'

'You better believe it,' Eddie said. 'If you'd been here earlier you'd have seen him cut the Buffer down to size. He has him eating out of his hand now.'

'You don't say? Sounds like I'm gonna have to watch myself, don't it?'

'Yes, Merv, I would if I was you. Take my word for it, he's very ruthless when people cross him or don't do as he says.'

'Well, I won't cross him then, but I would like to know why this bloke here is trying to hide under your skirt. Is he shy or what?'

I hadn't thought he could see over the desk. And when I stood up I was even more surprised that he could, for he was only a little runt with a sharp face and heavy-lidded eyes.

Eddie said, 'He used to be a detective.'

'Oh yeah?' he sneered. 'What's he doing here?'

It was time, I decided, to make my presence felt. 'I'm taking over from the Captain,' I snapped. 'That's what I'm doing here. Any objections?'

'Do us a favour, mate.' He said to Eddie, 'What happened to this hard case you said was moving in?'

Eddie seemed at a loss. 'That's him,' she sighed.

'Any objections?' I repeated.

The thin smile he'd been wearing broadened into a grin that bared his small brown teeth like a dog's snarl.

Eddie became more determined. Pushing her chair back, she stood up and said, 'You heard the man. Answer him.'

'Oh, I ain't got any,' he said, still grinning, 'but some of the others might.'

'In that case,' I said, stepping up to him and peering down into his hooded eyes, 'I'll just have to set a nice little example for them.'

'Set what you like, mister, but you don't cut no ice around here. If you know what's good for you —'

That's all he said, because at this point I socked him with a right hook just under his ear. He flew back against the wall, hitting it solidly on his side. Then with his cheek against it, his mouth still open, he started to slide slowly down until he was resting on his knees. With his right arm touching the wall, he stayed in that position for about ten seconds, just staring at the floor and trying to suck in some air.

I said, 'Any more lip out of you, buster, there won't be a skirt big enough for you to hide under,' and Eddie gave a little chuckle.

She said, 'You had me worried for a minute. I couldn't understand why you were letting that little fart talk to us like that.

'But I better warn you about him,' she added, putting her hand on my shoulder and whispering into my ear. 'He takes everything to heart. Now that you've hit him he'll always be looking for a way to get back at you.'

'Holds grudges, does he?'

'Yes, and he's as vicious as they come. You'll never be safe from him.'

'You mean I should take care of him properly? So as to have no more worries about him?'

'It's an idea.'

I think Merv must have heard us, for there was a very alarmed look on his face as he tried to push himself to his feet.

'Well,' I said, helping him up by his tie and slamming him against the wall, 'if you're gonna set an example you might as well do it right,' and with my other hand I pulled out the Colt 45 and shoved the muzzle in his mouth.

The poor sod was terrified. I don't think I've ever seen blood drain from a face as quick as it did from his. His eyes were as round and as big as pennies and from the side of his mouth a trickle of saliva ran over his jaw. He was shaking so much I could hear his teeth hitting against the metal of the barrel.

I glanced over at Eddie and she seemed to be all for it. In fact, judging by the flush on her face she seemed to be fairly enjoying herself.

I said, 'This is it, chum. I don't like doing it, but you've got to admit you didn't leave me much choice.'

He watched me hit the safety catch with my thumb then he made a last frantic effort to get away. But I had him well pinned against the wall and I just said 'Cheerio' and squeezed the trigger.

It went click, click, click as I squeezed it three times. Three small noises that rang out over the sounds of heavy breathing and Merv pissing himself. I said to Eddie,

'I took the clips from the magazine last night.'

'You might have told me,' she said, still staring hot-eyed at Merv's sagging head.

'You might have told me too,' said a voice from the door and I didn't have to look round to know that it belonged to the Buffer.

GETTING BIG LOANS
ON THE ISLE OF MAN

Things weren't looking too good for me at this point but I didn't even bat an eyelid. In fact, from the reflection of my gaunt face in Eddie's eyes I was too scared to do even that.

I stood there for a long, fragile ten seconds, just staring at a bald patch on Merv's scurfy head. Was this, I wondered in the rumbling silence, my last sight on Earth before the splitting crack of the Buffer's cosh or automatic? Was Eddie's whispered 'You've done it now, you stupid asshole' the last words I'd ever hear from the human voice?

No, there was no two ways about it. I was facing disaster in a seedy Paddington walk-up that said UNCLE TEDS TOYS LTD, and there wasn't a second to lose. I had to think fast and move even quicker. And that's why I made the mistake of grabbing Eddie by the neck.

'Back off, Buffer,' I hissed, leering over Eddie's shoulder as she stood unwillingly between me and the scowling hard-case at the door. 'I'm getting out of here and I'm taking this one with me. If you don't want her hurt you'd better step aside,' and I waved the Colt 45 at him for a bit more emphasis.

But the Buffer stood his ground. He wasn't carrying any weapons that I could see — he just stared at me with a great hate and slowly cracked the knuckles of his right fist into his palm. He wasn't making much noise, but it was louder than the traffic and the sound of little Merv standing up and moving quietly behind me.

Then the Buffer twisted his mouth in a kind of a grin and started to inch forward. The sound of his steel toecaps and heels grated on the wooden floor as he came slowly nearer. I think he was now enjoying himself. But as for me, I didn't like the situation one little bit.

Neither did Eddie. With a grunt, she rammed her elbow into my belly and I was as surprised as anybody when the gun gave a roar and almost jumped out of my hand.

There was a heavy smell of cordite, the back of Eddie's head cracked against my nose, Merv said 'Oh Jesus', and the shock on the Buffer's face was tremendous as he staggered back against the door.

After I caught my breath I let go of Eddie and put the gun in my jacket pocket. There was a trickle of blood running down into my mouth, so I took out my handkerchief and dabbed it dry before having a closer look at the Buffer, who was now sliding slowly down the door.

I said to him, 'You've a nasty burn on your neck, that's all.'

Eddie said, 'That shot'll bring the cops round here now.'

I said, 'You're right. We'd better make tracks.'

Merv said, 'I'd an idea that gun was loaded,' and started to shake his head.

I said, 'Makes you think, doesn't it?'

Then there was a groan from the Buffer and Eddie went over to help him up.

'I'm surprised at you,' she said when she'd got him to his feet. 'Getting on like that over a scratch on the neck. Makes me wonder what you'd have been like if he actually plugged you.'

'Big girl's blouse,' muttered Merv as he stepped up to open the door, still shaking his head. Then we all followed him out with the Buffer in disgrace bringing up the rear. We were in a bit of a hurry, so I was the only one who bothered to look back at the sign on the door which now read

CLE TEDS TOYS LTD.

I would have liked a body holster for that Colt 45, but the gun is so big it would have bulged out my coat too much. So I kept it in my jacket pocket even though Eddie told me to get rid of it. Of course, the reason she didn't want it around was that she'd used it herself on the tall heavy. But I explained to her that the cops wouldn't be able to prove anything now that her prints were taken off it, and she seemed happy enough about that.

But the rest of the gang didn't seem too happy when I pulled out the Colt 45 and placed it beside my glass of whisky on Merv's kitchen table.

Merv himself had to take a slug of his scotch as soon as he saw it, and the Buffer, who was stuck on a stool by the cooker, looked down at the linoed floor and started to rub his neck. The two other blokes, a bearded Jock called Archie and a darkey whose name I can't remember, exchanged uneasy bloodshot glances with each other. And when I got round to looking at Eddie, she gave a small sigh and there was a hint of exasperation in her dark, made-up eyes. But I just smiled and said,

'If the Captain gets himself lifted for fraud, he's only himself to blame. I told him before that he was only asking for trouble going around with Arab and American passports and getting big loans on the Isle of Man.

'The result of which,' I continued, catching a glimpse of Merv's bald spot in the OXO mirror on the wall, 'he's now somewhere in the Scrubs and he can't expect to run a firm from there. Now can he?'

There was a general agreement on this question and Eddie added,

'He almost botched that Oxford Street job too.'

That was a sore point with me, so I gave her a sharp tap on the ankle and said,

'Let's get down to business. What's this tickle you've been talking about down at the docks then?'

'Well, Barney,' she smiled, digging her stiletto heel into my toes, 'it's by no means a soft touch but I don't think it should cause you any bother. Merv got the idea when he was working down there a few months ago —'

I cut her short. 'Let's hear it from him then,' I said, annoyed at her calling me Barney, instead of Boss, after I'd done my damn'dest to get some respect from this crew. 'Come on, Merv, lay it out for us.'

116

Merv cleared his throat and went into a long drawn-out story about ripping off a bonded warehouse full of malt whisky due to be exported to Japan. It was dull enough the way he told it, but when Archie and his mate started questioning him on all sorts of minor details it became a real drag.

Still, I felt I had to show some interest, so I raised my eyebrows once or twice, nodded my head a few times, and amused myself by annoying Eddie with stealthy attempts to get my hand as far as possible up her skirt.

'Yes, that's all very well, Merv,' I said, watching myself light up a handrolled in the OXO mirror. 'But what are we going to do with the stuff when we get it?'

The little man looked lost for words, then he started to stutter.

'Or hadn't we thought of that?' I asked caustically. 'If you're smart enough you can pinch the Crown Jewels, but what are you going to do with them after that? Take them out each night and play with them?'

It was a good point because my first job after leaving school was smuggling a load of whiskey across the Irish border. The trouble was, I couldn't find enough publicans to buy the stuff and I was left with about ten crates which I kept under my bed. It took me over three years to drink that whiskey, just sipping away at the odd time and putting it in my tea. Of course, I was only young then. It wouldn't have been so much of a problem in later years.

Surprisingly, the Buffer decided to put in a word. 'We're okay there,' he said. 'My bruvver's manager of a booze wholesaler. He's done this before, Alf has.'

'That's alright then,' I said. 'As long as we can unload the stuff after we get it. Any more questions?'

'What about the fall-guys?' Eddie asked. 'We may have a problem there.'

I re-lit my handrolled. 'What do you mean, fall-guys?'

'Well, as you heard, they're a crucial part of Merv's plan —'

'Don't worry,' I said, intending to ask her about it later, 'that'll be taken care of. No need to concern yourself about that.'

I pushed back the chair and got to my feet. 'I mean to say, I wouldn't be much cop if I couldn't even produce a couple of fall-guys. Now would I?'

There was a strange silence for a few moments, as if I had said something remarkable, and then, all at once, they started to laugh. Even the Buffer. I didn't think it was that funny but I was glad, in a way, that the Buffer was getting his confidence back.

IT WAS ONLY WHEN I SAW THOSE RIDICULOUS HIGH-HEELS

Needless to say, I wasn't going to really use Petesy and Harriet as fall-guys on this caper. That would have been a very dirty trick to play on your mates. And besides, I never had the slightest intention of pulling off a job with Eddie's gang. I was only in with them for my own ends, and they didn't include a tenner in Wandsworth for a dockland heist. I mean, if I went inside over this warehouse job there wouldn't have been much left of me to come out again.

Anyway, the way Eddie explained it, Harriet was supposed to distract and drug the security guard while Petesy sneaked in and got nabbed by the pack of roaming Alsatians. The way would then be clear for us to cut the alarm system and make a hole in the fence big enough to drive the lorries through. According to Eddie, the Alsatians would be far too busy gnawing at Petesy to come near us and we'd have at least half an hour before the guard was due to make his regular call to head office.

Not the worst plan ever invented. But I couldn't see us getting in and out of there in under thirty minutes. So I decided to give Petesy and Harriet different instructions altogether. That way, when the job got all botched up I could say it was their fault.

I wasn't looking forward to seeing Harriet again. In fact, I had to tread very carefully in case she went berserk or even turned me in. But I had a little something in my pocket that would probably calm her down. It would probably make her agree to coming on the job too, not to mention giving me the coat back.

It was 10 p.m. I climbed up the fire escape and peered through the condensation on Harriet's window.

There was this curly-haired female lighting a king-sized with long red-tipped fingers. With smoke streaming from her nostrils she sat down facing me and I just happened to notice a chairful of dark-nyloned thigh that stood out forcibly against her frilled white blouse and red Minnie Mouse shoes.

In fact, it was only when I saw those ridiculous high-heels that I knew who it was. It was a new Harriet alright, dolled-up and permanent-waved into a very different proposition from the woman I used to know. I wondered what had got into her.

I rapped on the window.

Harriet uncrossed her legs and leaned forward. With her mouth open, she stared at me through narrowed eyes for about ten seconds. I rapped again.

'Open this window,' I mouthed, and made grating noises on the glass with my ring.

But she still didn't recognise me. So I took off my new snap-brim hat, my false moustache, and pressed my face against the window.

That did the trick. Stirring herself, she stepped over and pulled down on the sashes to let me in.

'The cops been here?' I asked, climbing down an armchair.

'Don't mention cops to me,' she snapped. 'And people have to sit in that chair, you know. Look at the gutters you've brought in with you. What's wrong with the door?'

'Here, Harriet,' I said, standing by the fireplace. 'I like that slit skirt of yours. It's about time you put on a show for your old man.'

'Don't flatter yourself. It wasn't bought with you in mind.'

I watched her flounce over to a small plastic radio sitting on the sideboard. To a background of a jazz piano, I said,

'Don't get the wrong idea about Eddie and me.'

She jerked round. 'Oh, she's welcome to you, Barney Huggins. The sort of her, she probably won't mind being turned over to the cops every time you need a patsy.'

She gave a bitter laugh. 'It shows how much you thought of me, doesn't it?'

'That's just where you're wrong,' I said, touching the box in my pocket that contained the engagement ring. 'Everything I did was for the eventual good of both of us.'

'Balls,' she said, twisting up her mouth.

This wasn't, I thought, the best time to make my

121

play. So I sat down by the smouldering fire and lit up a handrolled.

Harriet turned up the radio. I said, 'Since when have you liked that sort of music?'

'Since Arthur took me to a concert last night.'

'Where'd you find him?'

'In my wardrobe.'

It was a couple of seconds before I took that one in. 'Are you serious?' I cried, jumping to my feet.

'No, Barney!' she shouted as I dashed into the bedroom.

'Where's that bloody violin?' I roared at Manley, who was in the middle of putting on his green bow-tie.

'He doesn't have it,' cried Harriet, jumping on my back.

'We'll soon see about that,' I said grimly as I staggered towards the white-faced Manley.

'Leave us alone,' screamed Harriet, scratching my glasses off and then jerking back on my chin.

She cried out as we toppled over and there was a sharp pain in my hip as the pocketed Colt 45 smashed against Harriet's thigh. Then there was a blurred image of a boot on its way to make contact with my jaw.

I KISSED HER UNTIL HER FACE WAS RED

I was lying there with a sore hip, a dislocated jaw, and no glasses. All I needed now was to hear the cops running up the stairs and shouting 'We know you're in there, Huggins,' through the keyhole. It would have rounded an eventful day off nicely.

But I didn't waste time lying there feeling sorry for myself. I sat up, snapped my jaw back into place, and then crawled around the room looking for my specs. When I found them I picked up my hat and went into the living room.

As I'd expected, there was nobody there. I got out Harriet's bottle of whiskey from behind the Japanese firescreen and took long slugs from that. Then I set out to make sure the Strad wasn't in the flat.

I started in the bedroom and, needless to say, I

wasn't too worried about putting things back where I found them. Full of cold rage, I ripped and scattered as I went through the four small rooms, sparing nothing that could be cut open, broken, smashed or dented.

I destroyed her sofa, sideboard, armchairs, mattress, pillows and stove. I used a large clawhammer on her walls, floorboards, cupboards and electricity meter.

I found nothing whatsoever, and I left shortly before 11 p.m. with the feeling that I had probably burnt my boats behind me.

It's strange how things turn out. I'd gone to Harriet's with the intention of giving her an engagement ring and I ended up wrecking her rooms. The best part was that this ring business was originally a ploy, but after I saw how good she looked I began to think it wouldn't be such a bad idea after all.

I suppose I must have got carried away. But that's always a danger when the pressures of a case begin to close in on you. Your nerves become jangled with worry and booze, and you can't understand why the result of your enquiries is a complicated mess that seems to feed upon itself until you're reduced to making Harriet your fiancée so that (a) she'll allow you to take her fur coat away on the pretence of getting it drycleaned for the wedding, (b) she'll decoy and drug a security guard in order that you can gain entrance to a warehouse you had no intention of robbing in the first place, and (c) she'll give you back your Strad so that you can go on playing 'The Black Velvet Band' and 'The Yellow Rose Of Texas'.

I decided it was about time I took a cold, hard look at what was going on here. Things had got seriously out of hand and it seemed to me, as I sat sore and shivering on the bus to Eddie's new flat in Paddington, that I had only myself to blame.

Eddie lay back against the arm of the sofa and rubbed her stockinged feet along my thigh.

'How are we fixed for fall-guys, Barney?'

I finished off my glass of ale, leaving just a trickle of suds, and lingered over the beery fumes that rose from my mouth to the base of my nose.

'All set,' I said. 'Got us a pair of real experts.'

'That's good. We go tomorrow night.'

'Tomorrow night? I thought you said next month.'

'I did, but Merv says they're planning to ship the stuff out two weeks early.'

'That's a turn-up,' I said, wondering what was really behind this change of plan. 'Maybe we should call it off.'

'We could, of course,' Eddie yawned, 'but if you want to get in solid with the boys you'll have to show yourself capable of meeting these contingencies.'

Sometimes Eddie stopped talking down to me and used words like that. 'You're right, Eddie,' I said, stroking her foot, 'they have to be met sooner or later, these contingencies. I learnt that much in Korea. I'll never forget the day I came across two of them, Chinese they were, outside Pyongyang —'

'Another time, Barney. Who's doing the dirty work?'

'Petesy and Harriet.'

'Oh yes?' She showed me her top teeth, flecked with lipstick and framed in a long grin by full glistening lips. 'Still have a fancy for her, do we?'

'What do you mean?' I said.

125

'Just curious about that little sparkler in your pocket, that's all.'

'Look here, Eddie,' I said, 'I told you before not to go through my pockets. It's the worst of manners, so it is.'

'Don't change the subject. Who's it for?'

'Nobody. I'm selling it to this bloke.'

'I don't believe you. Oh Barney,' she grinned, 'don't tell me . . .'

'I'll tell you nothing of the sort,' I said. 'See that ring, I bought it off a gypsy —'

'Oh Barney, you mad romantic fool, I'll treasure it all the more.'

' 'Course, I knew it wasn't worth fifty quid, so I just looked him in the eye —'

'Show me, Barney,' she said, moving over and descending in my lap, 'show me how you looked him in the eye. Was it like this?' She fixed me with a wide-eyed stare. 'Or was it a much more mysterious gaze from the powers that lurk behind that battered and lovable front?' and she crossed her eyes until the pupils seemed to be looking at each other.

'So I just planted auto-suggestion in his mind that it was only worth a fiver — and the best part was, he never suspected a thing.'

'But neither did I,' she protested. 'All these years you never told me how you really felt, and poor little me, I never suspected a thing.'

I grabbed her hair. 'I'll suspect you alright, you sarcastic bitch,' and I kissed her until her face was red from my two days growth of stubble.

WHAT'S THIS ALL ABOUT, BARNEY?

'Alright, men,' I said, 'everything's taken care of. In exactly twenty minutes snip the alarm and get cracking.

'Archie, make sure there's a big enough hole in that fence before you and your mate try to drive the lorries through.

'Buffer, watch yourself with that sledge hammer. Give Merv a chance to work on the warehouse lock before you wade in with that thing. Above all, keep the noise down. Silence and speed are what we're aiming for here.

'Right, any questions?'

'Yeah,' said Merv, standing small and nervous against the high fence. 'Aren't you supposed to be coming in with us?'

'Come on, Merv,' I said patiently, 'use your loaf.

There's more to this job than just busting in there and grabbing a few crates, you know. Somebody has to supervise the fall-guys and watch out for the cops and make sure the escape route's clear.'

'But you said everything's been taken care of.'

'I also said how I take care of people who come up against me,' I told him, bulging out my jacket pocket with my hand.

Merv suddenly had no more questions, so I said, 'Just do your stuff and you'll be okay,' and strolled off in the direction of an alley that came up from the waterside and ended about twenty yards from the main gate.

'Alright, men,' I said to Petesy's shock-troops. 'Listen in. If I told you how much booze is in that place over there, you'd hardly believe me.'

'How much is there?' challenged the runt in the bush hat. 'More than the last time?'

'Wouldn't be in it,' I told him, putting it on a level he could understand. 'There's more there than the Bunch of Grapes could sell in a whole week.'

An impressed murmur came from the ranks. 'More than a pub's worth?' said the small troublemaker disbelievingly. 'Couldn't be. That's ridickleless. Do you take us for mugs or what?'

I held up my hand. 'That's alright then. I felt guilty about there not being enough to go round last time so I decided to treat youse all to a real drink. But if you're not interested —'

Several voices were raised to say that their owners were interested and Cecil, the troublemaker, was advised to keep his trap shut or else.

'I didn't say we weren't interested,' he protested meekly, having sidled back into the deeper darkness.

'But there is a snag,' I said regretfully. 'That bloke at the gate says we can't have our booze until next Monday when his boss comes back from holiday. Are youse prepared to wait until then, I wonder?'

As I'd expected, the shock-troops had no intention of waiting until next Monday. From their uproar of protest, faraway dates like next Monday could hardly be imagined, let alone tolerated.

'I can't argue with that,' I said and walked over to the ladder I'd left against the alley wall.

'I knew when I saw the ladder,' said the fat man smugly, 'that we'd be battering our way in again.'

'That's just where you're wrong,' I told him. 'This time we'll be using the ladder properly. In other words, we'll be using it to climb over the gate. You'll be holding it steady, and you' — I pointed at the other small size with golliwog hair — 'you'll be going over first, followed by Cecil and the rest of the squad. Any questions?'

Petesy himself put a word in. 'Only this, Mr. 'Uggins. Can I go now? I mean, I've got a very important appointment elsewhere at this moment and —'

'That's alright, Petesy. You've done your bit.' I slipped him a fiver. 'Off you go, old son. See you around.'

'Ta, Mr. 'Uggins,' he said with relief and set off down the unlit alley.

I looked at my watch. Zero hour was almost upon us, so I said,

'Right, men. Let's be having you. Take up your positions on this ladder and we'll have a bash at that gate.'

They'd had some practice at picking up and running with a ladder, so they eventually settled into their places with slightly less disorder than the last time.

'On the count of three. One ... two ... **wait for**

it . . . ' Cecil was trying to push one of the tramps out of the way so as to get at the front of the charge. 'Three!'

And so, with cries and wheeps and empty sherry bottles as clubs, the shock-troops assaulted the main gate.

I just stood in the darkness and watched their valiant attempts to raise the top of the ladder more than five feet from the ground.

It was a good question, I thought, whether they'd be attacking the dogs or the dogs them. And I definitely didn't give much for the chances of Buffer and his mates if they stood between the shock-troops and the booze.

But I didn't want to stick around for the answers to these interesting questions. So, whistling tunelessly to myself, I strolled off from the beseiged warehouse and made my way towards a bus stop.

It was the next day at Eddie's. I'd come back for my engagement ring. I'd unscrewed the lock from the door. I was hoping she was out. She was, but only down the hall having a bath.

I was hunting through her pockets in the bedroom when I heard the noise. You could tell Eddie's slippers a mile away. They were high-heeled and made a popping sound as the sole flew back against her heel. Sometimes I thought it was more like a flapping or even a sucking noise but at that moment, as I was trying to get under the bed, it came across very strongly as a popping sound.

The springs were too low to the ground so I crawled stealthily over the sticky lino and put my eye to the partially open door.

She nearly knocked my teeth out. The edge caught me on the side of the jaw, banging my head back. I had just started to feel the effects of that when she pushed again, this time clouting me smack on the nose. My chin dropped and I spent a short time in a ringing reddish haze before she added a few other colours with a savage shove that struck me on the top of my skull.

I was too punchy to shout out anything. I just crouched there on all fours, telling myself to get out of that place. It took me all of ten seconds before I thought of putting my hands against the door. Having done that, I tried to get to my feet.

I almost made it too. I was about halfways off my knees and halfways up the door. I was thinking she'd given up trying to barge her way in — she'd realised there was somebody there and was standing back, waiting for him to come out. I wasn't thinking she'd stepped back in order to get a good run at the door I was climbing up.

The lino didn't feel at all sticky when I hit it with my face. It felt more like a clash of cymbals with my head in between. It was worse than Manley's boot.

Eddie was towering above me, flapping the towel. It made waves in the air and strange swirling shapes. She was saying,

'What's this all about, Barney?'

I WONDERED WHAT REALLY HAD
HAPPENED ON THAT WAREHOUSE JOB

I said, 'It's usually the patient who's undressed, not the nurse.'

Eddie was dabbing up blood with the wet towel. It was brown and had the words SHARONS MOTEL printed on it. The last time I saw it was in my bathroom in Clapham. She shook her head.

'You're a difficult bloke to fathom, Barney.'

'What do you mean?' I said, reverting to my stunned state in order to avoid unpleasant subjects.

'You know right well what I mean. Why'd you do it?'

'Barney?' I said, gawking up at her. 'You called me Barney. Is that what my name is?'

'Come off it,' she snapped. 'I'm in no mood for this carry-on.'

'And I am, I suppose? Sitting here half crippled, with a sore mug, my tongue half bit off and a mind that's all a blur? I'm in the mood for carrying-on, am I?'

'Why'd you do it, Barney?'

She stood there looking down sternly at me as I made a series of faces to show I was racking my brain in a painful attempt to remember what she was talking about.

At this point the door opened and you can imagine my face when I saw the Buffer step in, rolling his shoulders and looking bigger than ever in a checked suit.

Merv was there too. He stood by the open door, peering down professionally at my handiwork on the lock. He said,

'Crude bit of work, that.'

I said to Eddie, 'What's he mean? Who are these chaps?'

The Buffer picked up my hat from the floor and sat it on my head.

'A bloody genius, that's what you are.'

The Buffer, I'd heard, liked a bit of sarcasm before he cut up rough.

Eddie said, 'He is, isn't he?'

I said, 'Look here, mates. There could be more to this than meets the eye, you know.'

Eddie gave a smile. 'You can say that again.'

Merv came over. 'You don't need to do that with those type of locks.'

I said, 'It's not easy trying to explain yourself when you don't have all your memory banks.'

Eddie tugged the towel up over her bust again.

'But when did you lose them? That's the question. They appeared to be all there when the job started.'

133

The Buffer seemed puzzled. 'What the hell are you lot going on about?' he said, looking at Eddie.

I looked up at her too, two large hurt eyes longing for an answer. Bewildered expressions come easy to a private eye. You just have to think of the way your last case ended.

But Eddie just smiled quizzically and said, 'A little misunderstanding, that's all.' She turned towards the bedroom. 'I gotta get dressed.'

'Well, that's alright then,' I said, rummaging through my pockets for a fag.

The Buffer shrugged. 'Where's the bar?'

'There isn't any,' Eddie said, and I gave a small jerk as she pushed open the bedroom door.

'You must have something,' the Buffer complained, looking round.

But he got no answer from Eddie. She had other things on her mind. Things I could only guess at as I sat there wondering why these two villains hadn't gone to town on me before now.

Merv said, 'What happened to your bonce? Run into a door?'

'Wish I could tell you,' I said, spitting out a small strand of tobacco.

'That's the worst of them handrolled. They go all mushy at the end and you can't keep 'em lit.'

The Buffer glanced over. 'Shows you've never been inside, mate. You'd soon learn to make 'em in there.'

I didn't know if he was talking to me or Merv. All I knew, it was just another small uncertainty in a very uncertain situation. There are special tactics to use in this kind of spot, but in my weakened state I couldn't remember them. All I could think of was making a dash for the door.

In fact, after listening to them going on for the next few minutes about fag papers, locks, getting bashed on the head and the absence of beer, I was almost wishing they'd say something about the job. Anything at all — threats, questions, accusations — just as long as it let me know where I stood. In other words, I was becoming a wee bit rattled.

But I didn't like it when Eddie came out wearing a tight black outfit and said,

'Well boys, what do you reckon Barney has coming to him after last night?'

'Where's the lav?' I said, springing out of the chair towards the door. And I would have made it too if my bad back hadn't give out as I leaped up, making me stumble and stagger with my spine bent over until I tripped over the shaggy rug by the door and fell very awkwardly with the handle nearly taking my ear off.

'For godsake, Barney,' Eddie said, standing over me with her hands on her hips. 'Will you leave those bloody doors alone? I'm trying to keep a low profile up here but it's not easy with you going around bashing into stuff like that.'

'Sorry, Eddie,' I said, suddenly feeling all the fight go out of me. 'I'll be quiet now. There's no need for any more of this. Just get it over with fast —'

'Oh, shut up,' Eddie snapped. 'We haven't touched you yet.'

'I don't understand this,' the Buffer complained.

Eddie kicked my foot. 'And get up off the floor. Go and sit over there while we discuss the job.'

'Discuss the payout, more like,' said Merv, rubbing his hands.

I caught Eddie's eye and she seemed to say, You lucky bastard, Huggins. So I got up and sat in an

135

armchair by the window. As I rolled up another fag I wondered what really had happened on that warehouse job. I looked up anxiously as Eddie plonked herself on the arm of the settee and said,

'Well, Barney, you surprised us all last night. From what I've been told, that was one hell of a diversion you arranged.'

'Too true,' muttered Merv.

Eddie crossed her legs and placed her hands on her knee.

'It seems that you were the only one who understood the weakness of the original plan. A small diversion wouldn't have given the boys enough time and — most importantly — it wouldn't have tied up the cops when they arrived. Also, I don't know how you knew there would be four security guards on duty, instead of the one we'd figured on, but that mob of yours took them in their stride.'

'Along with the dogs and the cops,' said the Buffer, nodding approvingly at me.

I snapped out of my open-mouth stare. I gave a small chuckle. 'Not to mention —'

'It was a bit strange,' Eddie continued, 'the way you cleared off in the middle of the job. That left us a man short for the loading. Not to mention,' she smiled, 'your behaviour here today. But I suppose that top-notch thinkers like you do tend to be eccentric at times.'

'I knew he was eccentric first time I saw him,' said Merv. 'When he was under the desk —'

'That's enough,' I snapped, my confidence now completely regained. 'Or maybe I'll remind you what happened after I came out from the desk,' and I glanced at Buffer as well, to make sure he remembered too.

Eddie shot me a look. 'You don't need to rest on those laurels any more, Barney.'

Which was a nice way of saying, Stop bullying the boys. But she didn't realise that a gang boss, even an eccentric one, has to reassert himself after he's seen whimpering at a broad's feet.

I ground out my butt. 'Let's talk about the take,' I said.

The Buffer looked thoughtful. Merv started to reckon up on his fingers, his mouth moving in time with the count. Finally he announced,

'Hard to say. Could be anything from ten to sixteen grand.'

I didn't know if that was, by gang standards, a good haul or not. So I just shrugged and said to Eddie,

'You sure there's no booze left?'

'See for yourself.'

'I will,' I said, and as I got up a shaft of pain shot through my back. I padded into her tiny kitchen like an old done man.

After I'd slammed a couple of cupboard doors Eddie came in and stood behind me.

'It's well seen,' I said, 'that you don't need a drink.'

As I tried to bend over to see what was under the sink, she placed her mouth against my ear and whispered,

'Barney Huggins, you are one hell of a lucky bastard.'

DON'T STOP NOW, EDDIE

I didn't think I was lucky at all. I hadn't wanted to go along with that dockland heist in the first place, and by employing the shock-troops I had only made things worse for myself. It was almost certain the cops had rounded them up, and effective as they were at storming places I could hardly imagine them crashing out of the nick or even sitting tight-lipped under fierce police interrogation, refusing stalwartly to put the finger on Petesy or myself.

Perhaps, I thought as I lay in the bath on Eddie's landing, I should go and see Sgt. Mungo. Tell him I was working undercover, explain about the warehouse job and how I tried to throw a spanner in the works. Which meant, of course, turning this lot in.

That idea didn't sit well with me, it was something I'd

seldom done before. But what can you do when you're looking at a long stretch in the slammer, like I was? After all, I reminded myself, I am a detective and that had to mean something when the crunch came.

But before I sent them over, there were one or two items of unfinished business I had to see to. I climbed out of the cold scummy water and stepped onto the lino. After a brisk towelling, I got into my togs and unsnibbed the door.

Eddie was still wearing her tight black number. It had seen better days but so had everything else in the room. It was split up the sides but not as much as the armchair she was filling, legs crossed, eyes following me as I went over to the window and checked once more for any suspicious cars or loiterers.

'Barney,' she said, 'how come you never take me anywhere?'

'What do you mean?' I said, lifting my gaze from the scene of the evening rush-hour traffic below.

'Oh, you know. Clubs, dancing, an evening at a smart out-of-the-way restaurant. And don't tell me you can't afford it yet. I've seen all those credit cards you have.'

'That sounds alright, but there are problems with those cards. They're not mine. Besides, we should be lying low, shouldn't we?'

'We can go somewhere outside London,' she said. 'I know the cards aren't yours but what difference does that make?'

'None, unless we're caught. I took them off Harriet to stop her using them. Are you talking about going to Luton or some place like that?'

'A likely story. No, I meant somewhere farther afield.'

139

'Up north, you mean?'

'Even farther. I was thinking of going abroad.'

'Abroad? You want to go abroad to go dancing?'

She sighed. 'Forget about that. I was only sounding you out. What I'm saying now is that we should get out while we can —'

'I've already come to that conclusion,' I said, not mentioning that I had other plans for Eddie.

'You have? How come?'

I sat down on the arm of her chair and lit a butt.

'Let's just say I've figured the whole thing out.' I spat a fleck of tobacco off my lip and then, smiling slightly, I gave a searching look that caused her to turn away and mutter,

'This should be good.'

'Look here, Eddie,' I said firmly, grasping her shoulder. 'I know the game's up too, but I'm not talking about rushing out and going abroad. What are you holding back from me?'

She shrugged. 'You know as well as I do how you made a balls of that warehouse job.'

'We got the goods, didn't we?'

'Sure we did. But the cops have got your mates, don't forget. That'll put them on to you.'

'Those men don't know my name.'

'They'll describe you. That'll be enough.'

'So it's me you want out of the way,' I said, jumping to my feet. 'And what's more, that's the way you always planned it.'

Her eyes flashed up at me. 'What's that supposed to mean?'

'Don't come the innocent with me,' I said harshly. 'You had me down as the chief fall-guy from the start. You had it all worked out —'

140

'Don't be ridiculous,' she snapped. 'Can't you see I've been protecting you? Have you any idea what the Buffer would do if I told him about your plan to sabotage the job?'

'Any protecting you've done,' I retorted, 'was to suit your own ends. Now that you've found I was too smart to carry the can, you're trying to scare me into running away without my share of the take. Well, let me tell you —'

'Barney,' she hissed, rising swiftly from the chair and standing with her face against mine. 'You're a bloody fool. You don't know one tenth of what's been going on this past few weeks. And if it makes you feel any better, neither did I until half an hour ago.'

As she made to turn away I touched her arm and said,

'Don't stop now, Eddie. What's been going on?'

'Listen,' she said in a tight voice. 'You're right about one thing: it was a set-up okay. But they were after me, not you. Oh, you were one of the smaller fish to be swept up in the net, and I dare say that would have given the Captain a chuckle or two —'

'Hold it,' I said. 'You mean the Captain's been behind this from the start?'

'Exactly. He told his barrister he'd just got wind of it, but it was him who arranged the whole thing. Then the barristers from both sides met the judge and it was agreed that the Captain had shown genuine remorse and was a great help to the cops. All he had to do now was plead guilty to the fraud charge and the judge would give him a suspended sentence. It's called plea bargaining.'

'So the Captain gets himself off and gets rid of you at the same time?'

'Neat, wasn't it?'

'But how'd he set up the warehouse job? I thought we planned that one ourselves.'

She smiled. 'So did I. But if you look back you'll recall that the original idea came from Merv —'

'That's right,' I said caustically, 'I should have shot him instead of the Buffer. I told you from the start the plan was hopeless. But you said I had to go along with it to get in solid with the boys.'

'Let me finish,' she said. Sighing, she lowered herself into the armchair and reached for her cigarettes. The lighter gave a tired click, she inhaled deeply, and a stream of faded smoke came out with her words,

'Merv's not the grass. Somebody else suggested the warehouse job to him, somebody who wanted to stay in the background so as to avoid being suspected later on.'

She gazed at me bitterly, inviting me to guess, and I had an anxious moment as the thought crossed my mind that all this was leading up to me.

'Surely you don't mean . . . ' I began, and as the words trailed away she started to nod slowly. She was like a bell tolling for the next customer of the Colt 45, and I felt my muscles tensing in readiness for a lunge.

'Yes,' she said, 'it was Archie all along.'

I let out the breath I'd been holding for extra springing power. 'That Scotch git?'

'The very one. I should have remembered how he was always sucking round the Captain, taking his side on every issue. A proper little toad, he was.'

'Has he scarpered?'

She shrugged. 'I don't know if he'll be there when we're supposed to hand over the booze.'

'When will that be?'

'Tomorrow night. The cops need a stronger case against me so they're holding back until the buyer

142

arrives to pay us and pick up the goods. They want to catch me on the premises, redhanded.'

'Who's the buyer? It's not Frankie, is it?'

She shook her head. 'Can't tell you that, Barney. I promised him I'd be the only one to know his name.'

'You going to warn him?'

' 'Course I am. There'll be nobody there when the cops arrive.' She smiled. 'Except Archie perhaps.'

'Well, at least you can tell us how you found out about this frame-up.'

She smiled again and made a sucking noise between her lips. 'Word from a judge, Barney. My own little man in the silver wig.'

I felt my mouth drop. 'You mean? . . . '

'That's right. I knew him straight away from that picture you took. Such a gentle old judge, and very eager to please too.'

'You certainly know your way around, Eddie,' I said, looking at her with reluctant admiration.

YOU'RE TALKING TO A DETECTIVE NOW

It was 7:15. I was sitting on a stool in the third pub down from Eddie's when I remembered the diamond ring.

I remembered it as soon as I looked in the bar mirror and saw my swollen nose, bruised cheek and the cut along the scar tissue above my left eye.

I was sitting hunched over with my chin in my hands and both elbows on the bar, a butt smouldering from my fist and my hat pushed back exposing the groove it had made in my forehead over the years.

It seemed an unlikely sight to remind anyone of a diamond ring. Yet it wasn't just the ring I was annoyed about, it was how Eddie could lower herself to take it from my trouser pocket while I was having a nap on her settee.

But I decided to leave Eddie alone until the morning.

My first priority was to put myself right with the cops. Explain to them it was the Captain himself who set up the dockland job, along with Archie and that barrister. They'd know that a private detective of my age doesn't suddenly start robbing warehouses. Even Sgt. Mungo would have to admit that it wasn't my form.

In a way, though, it was a pity I was leaving the gang so soon. Buffer and the rest of the boys would have come in very handy for getting my stuff back from Harriet. They'd have sent the wife back to Ireland with a flea in her ear too. And while they were at it, they could have called in for a chat with McConkey's wife and suggested she gave her boyfriends a rest.

Yes, even though I was in a tricky situation myself it still annoyed me that I'd let down old McConkey. I won't say I was a perfectionist but I always liked to be of some help to my clients.

But right now the only client I had was myself. So I had another short one for the road, paid a visit to the Gents, and then set off in the direction of Paddington tube station. I was on my way to Clapham in a black beard and a pair of rimless glasses with magnifying lenses which I normally used for searching and finding clues.

And it was a good job I had them on too, otherwise I might never have taken a closer look at that long-haired busker in an army greatcoat who was standing at the top of the steps in Clapham station.

There was a hat on the floor in front of him containing about 60p. But he wasn't going to get anything from me except a few tips on how to play 'The Kerry Dances', a tune which he brought to a screeching end after I'd passed him and was halfways down the steps.

I turned round and went back to him. I said,

'You'd do better if you held the thing right. Give it here a second.'

I put my hand out but he stepped back and growled,

'Keep your mitts off it. I know your tricks.'

'I only want to examine it,' I said, suddenly suspicious.

'Bugger off,'

I stepped closer, forcing him against the wall. 'That's enough of that. You're talking to a detective now.'

He snorted. 'Do us a favour, mate.'

I said, 'I know that violin. It's been stolen.'

'What makes you think that?'

'I have my reasons. Give it here.'

He shook his head. 'No way. Even if you was a real copper . . . '

Well, I couldn't delay much longer. A crowd might build up or some of his pals might come along to help him out. I couldn't risk snatching it in case it got broke. And I couldn't threaten him with the Colt 45 because Eddie had taken it back.

So I just gripped his throat with the first two fingers and thumb of my right hand, taking care to step to one side so he couldn't knee or kick me. Which was exactly what he tried to do, but after I tightened the vice even further he didn't bother with that anymore and just tried to slide down the wall. I was in an awkward position too, because I had to reach across my stomach with my left arm to keep a grip on the violin, and my right shoulder was hunched up against my ear in order to block out the busker's magnified face from the passersby.

'You son of a bitch,' I growled. 'Let go that violin or you'll be kicking your heels in hell before long.

Come on now, don't be a sap, gently does it.'

I kept up the pressure and then, just when I thought he was going to stiffen up on me for good, I felt his grip relaxing. Letting go of his throat, I reached down and the Strad came into my hands as softly as a piece of cake, bow and all.

But the busker nearly had the last laugh as he fell forward and clipped my elbow with his head. It was touch and go for a second as the Strad almost flew out of my grip, but with a bit of fancy footwork I managed to hold on to it alright. Then, without a glance in any direction but straight ahead, I marched off smartly, head high, with a faint rendering of 'The Marseillaise' playing on my bearded lips.

That's an unexpected stroke of luck, I thought, and the tonic effect of getting my Strad back stayed in my steps right along Clapham High St. and Driver St. until I reached the Bunch of Grapes.

It was half full. Petesy was sitting on his own in a corner. I bought two pints of bitter from an unsuspecting Emily and went across to him. He glanced up in surprise and said,

'I wondered what had become of you, Mr. 'Uggins.'

'No names, Petesy,' I said, sitting down facing him, my back to the bar. 'Can't you see I'm in disguise?'

He nodded. 'Right enough, Mr. . . .' then checked himself. 'What's it in aid of this time?'

'Don't you know?' I said with a strange mixture of surprise, disappointment and relief. 'Hasn't Old Bill been asking where I am?'

He looked thoughtful, rubbed his scrawny neck. 'Not that I know of. Not the law. 'Arriet has, though. She's been making enquiries, right enough.'

'And?'

147

'I said you'd gone to Australia, didn't I?' He drained his glass and reached for one of the full ones. ' 'Course, nobody believes that any more. I don't think nobody ever did. Couldn't we say somewhere more likely next time there's people asking for you?'

'Like the Scrubs, you mean?'

'I hope I never have to say that, Mr. . . . ' His voice trailed off but the glimmer of a smile remained.

'Did Harriet say why she wanted me?'

'Not 'alf she didn't. Told most of the pub about how this hard geezer came round looking for his fur coat. Apparently there was a bit of a battle and he duffed up 'Arriet and this Manley bloke who was with her.'

It was my turn to smile. 'You don't say?'

'Done them in proper too, from the look of her.'

I threw back the remains of my pint. 'I'll be on my way then. You sure there's been nobody else after me?'

'Far as I know there 'asn't . . . She's mad about what you did to her gaff too,' he added with a look of admiration. 'She said you've definitely gone too far this time.'

'Maybe I haven't gone far enough,' I said, getting to my feet. I dropped Petesy a couple of quid, told him to stay where he was for a couple of hours, then made my way unnoticed out of the bar.

REELING AGAINST THE FURNITURE IN
A VERY CONFUSED STATE

I said to Sgt. Mungo, 'I hear the wife's been making complaints about me again.'

He looked at me through narrowed eyes. 'Whose wife ye talkin' aboot?'

'Well, I suppose you could say it's mine. But the thing is —'

'That's no my concern. I never knew ye had a wife, God help her. Now go away heim, soldier, and stop wastin' our time.' He picked up some papers from the desk and glared down at them.

'That's alright,' I said. 'I just thought she was making complaints, that's all.'

'Well she hasn't.'

'And another thing —' I broke off as the sound of

heavy footsteps came down the hall from the 'interview rooms'. It was the young plainclothesman from the last time. He still had his hat on. He said,

'Don't I know you from somewhere?'

'You do,' I said. 'I was helping with the Oxford St. case. Any luck on that one yet?'

He stepped closer and poked my beard. All I could see was a gigantic nose. He said,

'This may seem like a stupid question —'

'It's Huggins,' the sergeant barked. 'He's under-cover.'

'What's he doing here?'

'Wife trouble, he says, but he's no sure.'

'It was over the head of this violin,' I explained. 'But I didn't kidnap anybody or shoot the tall heavy. Mind you, it was news to me the old Cap was plea bargaining. But it was still a good job I went through with it to make sure there'd be at least somebody on the inside. Wasn't I right?'

The young detective gave me a steely-eyed look, then he carried on past the desk and through the front door. I followed him out.

'See this violin?' I said, catching him up. 'You wouldn't believe it was a Strad, would you?'

Quickening his pace, he turned off into the station carpark. I stood there for a few moments, staring after him, feeling a brief silent chuckle.

I felt a little sorry for him too. It wasn't easy being a police detective, having to account for your time and having to make excuses to your boss about the unsolved cases. I was glad I didn't have a boss.

It was the next afternoon. I was calling on the Buffer. I'd

spent the night in Petesy's bedsitter. I'd bought him two bottles of Cyprus sherry so he'd make no objections. But after I'd seen the state of the place, I had to drink one myself as an anaesthetic.

The Buffer's house still hadn't recovered from the shock-troops but at least it didn't smell. He was lying on the settee in his vest, watching T.V. and sucking at a can of beer. I could have done with one myself. I said,

'What about this frame-up, then?'

'You know 'smuch about it as me,' he drawled. I didn't like it when he added, 'Maybe more.'

But I let it pass. I fired up a handrolled and said,

'Point is, do you believe it?'

'Bit dodgy not believing it, aint it?'

'You're right there. But couldn't we check it out somehow?'

'Suit yourself. Too dicey for me, though. Can't afford to take chances like that.'

'Of course you can't,' I said. 'Not after you've just come out.'

' 'Sright. Gotta watch meself.' He finished the beer then set about crushing the can into as small a shape as possible.

'Trouble is,' I said, watching him fold the can like a handkerchief, 'I don't know where we've stored the goods.'

He looked up, stared at me for a couple of seconds. Then his lip curled in a scornful smile.

' 'Sright. You don't, do you?'

He reached down for a beer on the floor beside him, his smooth-knuckled hand almost enveloping the can.

'All I need is for you to tell me,' I said.

There was a crack as he jerked on the tab. As he swung the can to his mouth a spurt of beer hit his cheek, ran down his bull neck and joined the other stains on his vest.

'Well? . . . ' I said, growing a bit impatient.

He looked up as if he'd forgotten I was there.

'What you say?'

'I want to know where the stuff is.'

'What for?'

'To make sure she's not conning us. You never know with her.'

He considered this for a second.

'My opinion, if you'd stuck around the other night like you were supposed to, instead of skiving off, you'd know where the bloody stuff is, wouldn't you?'

I was becoming mad now. I glared down warningly at him, but he was looking at the T.V., so I said gruffly,

'Look here, Buffer, I'd seriously advise you to come clean about where those goods are. You needn't think you can just lie there and talk to me like that.'

'What's that?' he murmured, his eyes still fixed on the screen.

I glanced over to see two young women playing tennis in the sun. The one with her backside to the camera had a skirt that wouldn't have covered my nose. You could just about hear the thud, thud, crack of the ball as they knocked it over the net. I crossed the room in four paces, timing it well so I didn't have to break step, and the T.V. made a kind of screeching sound as I put my foot through the screen.

Turning quickly, I took up a position with my left leg forward, my fists hanging loose at my sides, and said,

'What about it, then?'

The Buffer's face was a picture in itself. He was even more surprised than when I pulled the gun on him at UNCLE TEDS. He'd thought he was dealing with a spent force, but I'd just shown him different. I'd just put my foot through his T.V., I was all braced up ready to tackle him next, and I wasn't leaving until I got some answers about the warehouse job.

I braced myself even further as he threw the beer can to the floor and got slowly to his feet, a vicious glare burning in his eyes. As he moved deliberately towards me he rolled his shoulders, loosening them no doubt for a fast combination of blows to my body and head. His lip was curled in a slight smile, his breath came loud, wheezing, and his normally blotched cheeks were drained of blood, a pale mass of tiny holes and pock marks.

His left came up like a massive twitch and I reacted instantly by stepping in and blocking with my right, my own left hook already on its way. But he'd only feinted and my guts caved in as his right rammed home below my ribs. I almost blacked out, but as the force of the punch sent my head and chest jerking violently forward I managed to block the follow-up, a right uppercut to the chin, by butting him on the nose with my forehead.

It must have stunned him, for he stepped back with a dazed look in his eyes, and I took a couple of seconds myself to see if I could get my breathing started again.

Then I went on the attack, unleashing my own combination at his temple and chin. But I was very stiff from my injuries over the past week and my punches, lacking their usual snap, did little more than glance off the top of his lowered head.

So I stepped back to get a good kick at his knee, and as I did so there was a loud crack as his right landed flush on my jaw.

It was sore alright, and the force of it had me reeling against the furniture in a very confused state. But it

153

wasn't my jaw that was broken, it was the Buffer's hand. He'd hit me plump on the steel plate the surgeons had used to replace part of my jawbone.

When I'd steadied up and got him back into focus he was swooping down to pick up a poker from the grate. Now, even one-handed, I knew he'd wreck me completely with that poker, so I risked everything by rushing at him and going into a flying leap just as he straightened up to face me.

My feet caught him somewhere in the midriffs and as they connected I brought my hands and forearms down to take the force of the landing away from my back. I heard him crash into the fireplace, a cry, a grunt, then a crack as the poker fell onto the tiles.

By the time I was able to sit up, the Buffer was already stirring, his hand just starting to move across the tiles. So I pulled the poker from his reach and pinned him to the floor by forcing it down on his throat. Kneeling over him, I said breathlessly,

'Ready to talk now, are we?'

He was beaten alright, but he still managed to include a lot of resistance in the glare he was giving me. So I slapped him about the chops a few times, repeated the question, then slapped him some more.

'Where's those bloody goods? Come on, Buffer, speak up.'

But there was no talking to him. He became more stubborn by the minute. It was clear he'd no intention of letting on where the stuff was. I was only wasting my time.

I stood up. My mouth had filled with blood again. I spat it over him and said, 'I'll settle with you later, bub.' I picked up my hat and crossed to the door. I turned, he was still lying there. I said 'Yah' to the whole scene then I went out.

I wanted a drink, but there wasn't a moment to lose. As I walked to the tube I lit up a handrolled, sucking the smoke in greedily through my bloody mouth. Whenever anybody got in my way I just pushed them aside.

When I reached the station I found I'd no change, so I just barged on past. At the other end a black geezer demanded a ticket off me, so I just put my hand on his face and pushed him back into his chair.

I trudged up the stairs, along the landing, banged on Eddie's door. The lock was still broken and it swung open. When I saw she'd done a bunk I started to eff and blind. I stormed into the bedroom and flung open the cupboards. But apart from a lining of yellowed newspapers, they were as empty as a whore's promise.

THIS HAS GONE FAR ENOUGH

I'd got the rough end of the stick right through this case, but I think the real low point came when I arrived back at Petesy's place.

As I stepped into the fusty, junk-filled room, all the events of the past two weeks seemed to gang up and hit me. I started to shake a little, my legs went weak, and I felt like throwing myself on the bed and having a bloody good cry.

There were two old typewriters on the bed, plus a pair of Wellington boots. I hadn't the energy to shift them, so in one sweep I cleared the armchair of a pile of fiftyish detective magazines and slumped down in it.

I sat there for a long time, just chain-smoking and thinking tired, sour thoughts. Every five minutes or so a little bird from one of the three cuckoo clocks on the wall would shoot out and I would think about getting to my feet, stepping over several piles of rubbish and reaching up to stop the pendulums.

Finally I fell into a doze. When I woke up it was almost dark. The room smelt slightly different, a mixture of cigarette smoke, fusty junk and Petesy. I pushed up the brim of my hat and peered into the gloom.

He'd been there alright, I could tell by the way a path had been cleared to the window. I sat up and rubbed the stiffness and pain out of my neck. As I did so, I wondered what he was trying to see out of that window, which looked onto a narrow unlit alley. It seemed strange he could have come in and moved that stuff without waking me. He must have been deliberately quiet, I thought as I eased out of the chair and took careful steps towards the window.

And sure enough, standing at the mouth of the entry was a shapeless figure, its back against the wall, its face concealed by shadow and a hat pulled down over one ear. The tip of a cigarette glimmered in its hand and as I watched, it came slowly up to the lips, glowed brightly for a second over a tough profile, then was flung in an arc to the ground.

Yes, it was Harriet alright, and it took me about five seconds to stumble out of the room and reach the top of the tight stairs, which I almost fell down owing to the lino being broken and turned up. But I grabbed hold of the bannister, and after a nasty moment when that creaked and moved like it was going to give way, I steadied up by throwing myself face down over the top step and forcing my hands against the wall and the base of the bannister.

It was a sore thing to do, though a lot better than tumbling down the stairs. But when I tried to get up I

157

found I'd jammed myself too much. My arms wouldn't budge on account of them being crossed under me and I had a strong suspicion my back had given way too.

So I just lay there, looking down the stairs, trying to force my shoulders up, and hoping that the footsteps clacking along the front of the building didn't belong to Harriet.

I lay perfectly still as the door opened with a groan and a head in a distinctive felt hat protruded into the hall. There was still a chance I wouldn't be noticed, but it faded pretty fast as Harriet crossed to the stairs and placed her foot on the first step.

As she came up towards me I made a last desperate struggle to lift myself off the floor. And I would have made it too if she hadn't rushed up the last few steps and forced me down with her foot between my shoulder blades.

That was bad enough, but what really hurt me was when she put her hand on the wall and carried on walking over my back. The pain was terrific, particularly on the spots that were already sore, and I felt all sorts of things breaking, tearing, or being crushed.

There was no chance of me getting up now, so I just lay there with my head hanging over the top step until my hat went tumbling down the stairs. I was cursing and moaning and gasping as the spurts of pain ran into each other, banging together in a framework of sheer agony. I thought it was very mean of Harriet to have done a thing like that.

In a couple of minutes she came back and started to stomp over me again. I cried,

'For godsakes, Harriet, you've banjaxed me enough as it is.'

But she just carried on completely wrecking my back.

'I think I deserve this,' she said, sitting down on the steps below my head.

I wasn't sure if she meant the punishment or the Strad she was balancing on her knee. I said,

'Look here, Harriet, this has gone far enough —'

But she had pulled a ball of tissue paper from her pocket and shoved it in my mouth.

'You got off light, son,' she said, pushing my chin up with her finger. 'You're not worth a shit, but at least you never sunk as low as that fucker Manley. He just sat there cringing while this heavy gave me a bashing because I wouldn't hand over the coat. It was a present from a detective, I told him, who'd be very upset if he ever laid his paws on it. But he just sneered and cuffed me some more, then he started in on Manley and nearly choked him senseless with his green bow tie.'

She stood up, and there was a trace of affection in her eyes as she bent over and ruffled my hair. But as I watched her Minnie Mouse shoes clump down the stairs, I was already planning my revenge on Harriet. Not to mention Petesy, Eddie, and almost everyone else connected with the case.